Jake reac[hed] [for her at] the same time her foot slipped on the running board.

She fell forward against him. He caught her against him, feeling her arms clasp around his neck for support. The soft smell of strawberries wafted up from somewhere. He looked down into her deep green eyes and saw her hint of dismay.

Then it registered what else he was feeling— her stomach?

His eyes widened, and he looked down. Sure enough. Though they were touching in the middle, the rest of her body came nowhere near his.

Totally surprised, he looked back into her eyes and said, "You're pregnant."

Books by Cheryl Wolverton

Love Inspired

A Matter of Trust #11
A Father's Love #20
This Side of Paradise #38
The Best Christmas Ever #47
A Mother's Love #63

CHERYL WOLVERTON

Growing up in a small military town in Oklahoma where she used to make up stories with her next-door neighbor, Cheryl says she's always written, but never dreamed of having anything published. But after years of writing her own Sunday school material in the different churches where she's taught young children, and wanting to see more happy endings, she decided to give it a try, and found herself unable to stop.

Seeing so many people hurting, afraid to reach out and accept God's forgiveness, inspired her to begin writing stories about God's love and forgiveness in romances, because, she says, "We can't truly have happily ever after if we don't have that happily-ever-after relationship with God, too."

Cheryl now lives in a small Louisiana town and has been happily married for fifteen years. She has two wonderful children who think it's cool to have a "writing mama." Cheryl loves to hear from her readers. You can write to her at P.O. Box 207, Slaughter, LA 70777.

A Mother's Love
Cheryl Wolverton

Published by Steeple Hill Books™

STEEPLE HILL BOOKS

Steeple
Hill™

ISBN 0-373-87063-9

A MOTHER'S LOVE

Copyright © 1999 by Cheryl Wolverton

Look us up on-line at: http://www.steeplehill.com

Printed in U.S.A.

He shall call upon me, and I will answer him:
I will be with him in trouble; I will deliver him,
and honour him.

—Psalm 91:15

To Marcia Bender, who was the first to ever tell me how much she loved my books. This one's for you. Thank you to Donna Blacklock and Denise Gray, who have supported each and every book I've written with book-signings and encouragement and who were both enthusiastic when I told them about this one. You'll never know how much that means. And to my sister, Deborah. I love you, hon. I hope this one touches your heart, too.

Prologue

❧

Maggie looked at the suitcase sitting by the front door. It didn't contain much, just her most treasured possessions. Funny how everything she really cared about could fit into one suitcase.

Looking back at the house and the lavish staircase, she realized what a pampered life she'd led.

Fear clutched her heart, emerging from her numbness. So much had happened in the past seven weeks, things that had totally changed her outlook on life. No more was this house a haven for her; no more was it a place she could run to when she was hurt or afraid.

She saw a maid peek around the corner, heard the muffled sniffles of another when she picked up her suitcase. Maggie hadn't realized how much the staff cared for her. Of course they wouldn't say anything about her leaving. Their jobs wouldn't permit it.

Had her whole life been so marked by privilege?

She'd been so innocent, working at a job that had been provided for her, going to the church where she'd been raised, doing everything she'd always been told.

Until now.

But she just couldn't do what her parents had asked of her.

She couldn't.

At twenty-six, she was old enough to make her own decisions. It was time to stop listening to everyone else. *Past time.*

So, when the ultimatum had been given, she had shocked everyone by accepting it.

She went to the door, then looked back one last time. Black dots danced before her eyes, and she swayed before fighting off the dizziness. She'd never been on her own before. She was scared, more scared than she could ever remember being. She took a deep breath.

Pushing the desolation from her thoughts, she reached for the brass doorknob and pulled the door open. She wished once again there was an easy way out of the mess she was in.

But there wasn't. That was why she was leaving.

For better or worse, she had made her bed; now she had to lie in it.

Squaring her shoulders, she headed toward the cab, refusing to look back, promising herself to only look ahead. She would rely only on herself from this day forward to get herself through the next six months.

Chapter One

"Shirley quit?" Jake Mathison swerved to avoid a huge puddle in the middle of the road, the beat-up truck bouncing as he hit a pothole instead. He moved the cell phone from his ear, then brought it back. "But she was assisting with those plans we've been working on as well as keeping my notes. And," he suddenly added, "she helps with the children's programs."

Doom loomed before him as he realized all that would be left hanging with Shirley gone. He almost missed Jennifer's next words, but instead nodded with exasperation. "I know, Jennifer. I'm not blaming her. If Charlie finally asked her to get married, I can see why she jumped at it. She's been head over heels in love with him forever. I even counseled her when he left. That's why she took that vacation out there." Jake now wished in a small way that he'd had her wait just a bit longer.

No, that wasn't true. He was happy for her.

He listened as Jennifer quickly suggested a solution.

"Yeah, okay. You do that. Maybe if you put it in the church bulletin, someone will be interested in temporarily assisting me."

Though it was the middle of the afternoon, Jake squinted through the deepening gloom that had settled over the small streets of Centerton, Louisiana. It was the time of year for hurricanes. And whether they had hurricanes or not, the summer months always brought rain. So what if today was like a monsoon? Yesterday had been, also.

"Yeah, Jennifer. No, I won't be back today," he replied to her question. "Go on home to Gage."

He squinted again as he went down the country road. "You, too. Bye." He hung up.

Jennifer was a wonder. He adored her, had been delighted when she'd come to work for him as the day-care manager at his small church. Jake had even performed her marriage ceremony six months ago. He depended on her help.

Just as he had Shirley's.

So, what was he going to do without his assistant? Not only had she kept his files in order, helped him when he went on his children crusades into the inner city, but she'd also been working closely with him on his latest project: getting the cities around Baton Rouge to pitch in and work together to build an inner-city recreation center where the kids would have a place to go, to get off the streets and away from drugs.

And now Shirley was gone.

Maybe it was the rain or his telephone call that kept him from seeing the woman until he was right beside her.

He caught only a flash of someone with long limp hair, huddled in an oversize yellow raincoat, before his truck splashed her and she cringed.

He hit the brakes, pulling off the road immediately. In his rearview mirror he saw the person stumble and fall from trying to avoid his splash.

"Oh, great! Good going, Jake," he berated himself. He grabbed his umbrella and ran back to where the young girl was struggling up. Concerned, he held the umbrella out over her, trying to protect her from the rain.

Reaching down, he extended his hand. "Are you okay?"

The girl placed her pale-white hand in his. He felt calluses on the pads of her fingers, saw short clipped nails that were clean of nail polish. She struggled up.

When she lifted her head, green, the brightest he'd ever seen, met his gaze and he was transfixed. This girl—*no,* he corrected himself, *this woman,* had the most exquisite eyes he'd ever seen. They were beautiful. Large and innocent, they were framed by dark lashes. Perfectly arched eyebrows, a darker shade than her eyelashes, crested over her eyes. A few small freckles dotted the bridge of her nose, the same color as her dripping red hair.

Then her expression changed, became guarded,

world-weary. "Are you okay?" he repeated, wondering what had caused the change.

"Fine."

He waited, but she didn't say anything else.

"Can I give you a ride somewhere?"

She started to shake her head, but he stopped her. "It's pouring rain. Come on. I can't leave you out here like this."

She lifted her chin, then sighed, her shoulders drooping.

What could make this beautiful woman look so beaten down? His heart went out to her. "It's okay," he reassured her. "I won't hurt you. Besides, it's the least I can do, since I wasn't paying attention and splashed you."

She raised her wary gaze to his again, then nodded once, curtly. "Thank you."

He walked beside her to the car. "I'm Jake Mathison."

"I'm Margaret…" She hesitated.

"Margaret? You look more like a Maggie," he joked, trying to put her at ease as he opened his truck door.

She lifted astonished eyes to him.

"You *are* a Maggie." Jake laughed, knowing he'd guessed right, and her gaze softened for just a minute.

"I'm sometimes called that," she finally replied. She turned her back on him and climbed into the cab.

He wished he'd brought his car, but he'd had to do some errands for the church. Though his congregation ran just over one hundred now, it didn't seem as if he ever had enough help.

Going around, he hopped in the driver's seat. "Well, Maggie, where can I take you?"

"My car is about two more miles down the road. I need to stop and see if I can figure out what's wrong. If you'll just drop me off there…"

He looked at the hat—the one with the familiar logo—she was wearing on top of her sodden curls as he pulled back onto the highway. "You work at the fast-food restaurant about five miles back?" he asked.

"Umm-hmm," she said, staring out the window, not meeting his eyes.

So, she didn't want to talk. But Jake couldn't let it go. He was concerned. She shouldn't be out walking the streets, especially in a rainstorm. "You on your way to work?"

Another sigh escaped her, and then he saw it. One lone tear slipped from her eye and trailed down her cheek, mingling with the wetness already there.

Uh-oh, he thought. *Help me, Father.*

Very softly he said, "You want to talk about it?"

She shrugged.

He didn't push her but waited.

Finally, she said, "I was at work, but they let me go."

He drove along the bumpy road, doing his best to avoid potholes. Jake wondered if she saw the green trees lining the highway or if she was simply looking inside herself at something he couldn't see. He was almost certain it was the latter.

"You were late because of your car?" he prompted.

She shrugged. "That was only an excuse. It doesn't matter," she added, suddenly sounding stronger. "I don't need anyone. I'll find another job."

They arrived at a broken-down, rusted-out yellow compact. She started to get out. Jake touched her arm to stop her but wasn't prepared for her reaction.

She jumped and jerked her head around. Fear flashed through her eyes, before warning replaced it.

He immediately pulled back, giving her space.

"I'm an old hand at working on cars. Let me have a look at it."

"It's not necessary—"

"Think of me as a knight in shining armor," he teased, smiling at her. "My mama would come back from her grave and tan my hide if I left a lovely woman like you stranded with a broken-down car."

The first smile he'd seen cracked her lips. It transformed her face, made her eyes look even greener.

Oh, boy, he thought, stunned by her effect on him.

He quickly exited the car. Going over to the compact, he popped the hood and looked under it. "Uh-huh, here's your problem," he said, fingering a belt. "I have a friend who owes me a favor. What say you let me have your car towed to your house, and I can fix this for you?"

She stiffened. "I don't think so. I'll take care of it myself."

Puzzled by the sudden anger in her eyes, he wondered what he'd said. "I've got a cell phone in the truck. Just hang on...."

"I can't pay for the repair," she finally confided, lifting her chin haughtily.

Realizing she was embarrassed, he smiled. "There's no charge. Like I said, he's a friend and I'll put the belt on for you. The belt is only a couple of dollars."

"I can't ask you—"

He strode back over to her, touching her shoulders. Her arms felt small through the slicker.

When she stiffened again, he immediately let go. "You aren't asking me for anything. But there's no way on this earth I'm leaving you out here in this downpour to get soaked."

He turned, swiped a hand at the rain pouring down his face, then went back to his truck to make a call. By the time he was done, the rain had almost quit.

And Maggie was again looking nervous. When he walked up she surprised him. Instead of trying to talk him out of helping again, she offered a tentative smile. "Thank you."

"You're welcome."

"Your friend doesn't mind getting out in this?" she asked, looking up at the sky.

He smiled. "Nah. He's a good guy."

She had the front of his truck between them, and he allowed it. After all, he was a stranger. It was only right that she be cautious. He wanted to reassure her but wasn't sure how to put her at ease. The road was deserted, lonely. She had a right to be wary.

"Am I keeping you from something?"

He smiled, trying to help lessen the tension. "No, ma'am. As a matter of fact, I was just on my way home."

"Do you need to call your wife or something?"

His grin widened. "No wife or something. No relatives at all."

She ducked her head.

Interesting.

He sidled over to front of the truck. "Have you lived here long?"

She shrugged. "Two months."

"I bet you live in the trailer park about two more miles up the road."

She looked up, surprised.

He answered her unspoken question. "It's the only thing up the road besides the church and a couple of subdivisions."

"How do you know I don't live in one of those subdivisions?" she asked.

"I don't. But the hat you're wearing wouldn't pay the rent on those houses. Unless you're independently wealthy and just work at the fast-food restaurant for fun."

She opened her mouth to comment, when suddenly her stomach growled.

Red crawled up her face to her hairline.

He grinned. "My stomach's telling me the same thing."

Her lips formed a small smile again. "I get hungry a lot."

The sound of a truck caught their attention, and

they turned. Jake was relieved. He'd never had such a stilted conversation in his life. He was down-to-earth, always putting everyone at ease. This woman had a wall thicker than the Great Wall of China built around her. "That's Tyler. Go ahead and get in the truck. We'll hook your car up and then you can give us directions to your house."

He started to walk off, but the woman called his name.

"Yes?" he asked, turning.

"When we get to my house, I'll be glad to feed you dinner for your help."

He could tell that offer cost her a lot. Still, he was glad for the invitation. He nodded. "That's very nice of you, Maggie. Go on, now. Get in the truck. I'll be right there."

"She sure is a pretty little thing," Tyler said as Jake walked up. He and Jake worked on getting the car hooked up to his truck.

Jake glanced back to see the woman sitting alone in the dilapidated old truck. "Yeah, I suppose she is." He remembered the haunted look in her eyes.

"So she's caught your eye, has she?" Tyler joked.

Jake turned back around and chuckled. "How could she not? She's beautiful." It was the honest truth. He saw no reason not to admit that to Tyler. But he didn't mention there was something more than beauty that had snared his attention. He couldn't quite put his finger on it. Maybe it was the simple fact that she needed someone, and Jake was the giving type.

Tyler laughed. "I'm surprised you even noticed."

Jake raised an eyebrow, then chuckled. "I've dated, Tyler. You know that. I just have too much to do and no time to go looking."

"I know other preachers who've gotten married," Tyler replied, going around to the other side of the car.

"I have, too. Some of them are my friends. But the right woman has just never come along."

He finished adjusting the chains, then nodded. "Follow us. Maggie said she'd give me directions."

"Sure thing, Jake," Tyler said, and headed toward the truck.

Jake went back to his truck. *Marriage.* Now, where had that come from? He supposed many in his congregation wondered why he'd never married. He was finally realizing a lifelong goal in his inner-city ministry program. He honestly didn't believe he had time for marriage with all that going on. Or he, at least, had no time to look.

"It shouldn't take too long," he said, turning his attention to Maggie when he got in the truck. He was pleased when she smiled....

He started the truck. "Which way?"

She pointed one long slender finger. "You were right about the trailer park. If you turn in the second entrance, I'm the first trailer on the right under the big oak tree with the long patio porch."

"So," he said, pulling back out onto the highway, watching as Tyler slowly followed, "do you have any new job prospects?"

If she thought his question too personal, she didn't show it. She only shrugged. "I'll find a job."

"What type of work do you do?"

If he hadn't chosen that moment to glance at her, he was certain he would have missed the flash of bitterness in her eyes. As it was, she covered it quickly. "I do a bit of everything. I've done inventories, was an executive secretary, a cook, fast-food."

Surprised, he asked, "Why aren't you in Baton Rouge looking for a job? Executive secretaries make much more than a fast-food restaurant worker would."

"There are no openings where I applied. Besides, I have no references."

An idea formed. He had to tread carefully, though, because he didn't want to push Maggie the wrong way. "Have you ever worked construction or anything like that?"

She didn't answer.

Oh well, it had only been a hope. He'd been lucky that Shirley had experience in that area. Still, maybe if this woman could just keep good notes...

"I worked in a building company," Maggie said, breaking into his thoughts. "I did everything from dealing with the people who ordered lumber to talking with people who were building their own houses. I loved that. I thought, at one time, building would be my future."

She had a distant look. He wondered what experience from her memories of that job had to do with the lingering pain in her eyes. He couldn't help but ask, "Why aren't you still there?"

Maggie snapped back to the present, the wary look

returning. "No reason. Why are you asking me all these questions?"

He smiled. "I just might know of a job."

He turned in to the trailer park. "But why don't we talk about that after I get your car fixed, okay?"

"Sure," she said.

He didn't hear much hope in her voice, though.

"It pays better than a fast-food restaurant, and I think you'll be perfect," he added, and was glad he did when he saw a small spark of hope in her eyes.

"I'll go fix dinner," she said. "If you'll excuse me…"

Jake turned off the engine and slipped out. After going around to her side of the vehicle, he opened her door to assist her down. "I appreciate the meal. Watch your step here," he warned, realizing he'd parked in a huge puddle.

Jake reached up to help her at the same time her foot slipped on the running board. She fell forward against him.

He caught her small body against his, feeling her arms snake around his neck for support. The soft smell of strawberries wafted up from somewhere. He gazed into her deep-green eyes and saw her hint of dismay.

Then it registered what else he was feeling.

His eyes widened, and he glanced down. Sure enough. Though they were touching in the middle, the rest of her body came nowhere near to touching him.

He thought of the pictures of starving kids in Africa but of course knew that wasn't her problem.

Totally surprised, he looked back into her eyes and said, ''You're pregnant.''

''Gee,'' she replied, roughly, her eyes brimming with sudden defiance and a cynical smile slowly twisting her lips, ''what was your first clue?''

Chapter Two

Totally surprised, she looked on Kevin because
and with his expression a more ...
"He's ... she called out, an ... most sh...
with sudden silence, and a frantic swing ...
evening her legs," with, and went but ...

Chapter Two

"I'm so sorry. I didn't mean that the way it sounded."

Maggie shrugged. "No big deal," she said. And it wasn't. She had no business thinking of this man the way she had been thinking of him.

"Go on and fix the car. I have to prepare dinner."

She walked off, leaving him standing there gaping. No wonder he'd been so nice to her, she thought dispiritedly. He hadn't realized she was pregnant. How could he have missed it?

After unlocking the dead bolt, she went inside before pushing the metal door closed behind her.

Wearily Maggie took off her raincoat and her shoes. She was soaked. She went to the bathroom, grabbed a towel to dry her hair, then combed the long curly red strands before clipping it back out of her face with a large clasp. Gazing at herself in the mirror, she realized she looked tired. Purple circles shadowed her eyes.

She'd get some sleep tonight, she vowed. No more nightmares.

She changed into a blue summer dress with flowers. She'd found it at a secondhand store. "Beggars couldn't be choosers," the saying went. And it was true. She'd learned a lot about shopping and buying things she wouldn't necessarily have ever considered before. However, the dress looked okay on her. She would have preferred green or black, but blue it was.

Maggie pulled on a pair of fuzzy slippers. With a long sigh she pushed herself up and then padded back into the kitchen to see what she had to fix.

She wondered if Jake was still out there, or if had he run as soon as she was out of sight. He'd been shocked enough to want nothing more to do with her.

Pulling back the flowered curtain, she peeked out the kitchen window. Nope, he and his friend were still there, working on her car, talking—probably about her. Slightly curly, dark-brown hair was slicked down against Jake's head. His wide shoulders blocked out most of the engine as he pointed to something and motioned at Tyler.

When he'd first stopped she'd been frightened. Of course, that was a leftover from the past, from things she tried to forget. Since she knew what an acquaintance could do to a woman, a stranger automatically made her nervous. People didn't really help other people. She didn't believe it.

But Jake had been willing to help her.

She still couldn't get over how friendly he had

been, or how willing to help. She knew nothing about him. He didn't know her, yet he'd pulled more information out of her than anyone else had over the past six months.

He was easy to talk to. Too easy.

And she'd been glad to have him there. That had made her automatically nervous. She didn't need anyone. She'd learned that, and she wasn't about to risk it now. But if she decided to take a chance, she thought, glancing out the window again, she'd definitely want it to be with him.

He certainly was gorgeous, she acknowledged as she watched him stand up straight. Tall, a good six inches taller than her, and strong. He'd held her above the ground a minute ago while staring into her eyes as her condition dawned on him. He hadn't acted as though she weighed anything. But where strength had scared her before, it was strangely reassuring when coming from the man with the gentle eyes. While her heart had been tripping over a surprising attraction, his had been recoiling at his discovery.

Her cheeks burned with embarrassment. It had to be her hormones that had made her react to the man.

Maggie opened her cabinets, trying to figure out what to fix. It'd been a while since she'd cooked. She was very careful and rationed her food to make it last. Two bags of egg noodles, one larger bag of spaghetti noodles, four cans of tomato sauce, various spices, six macaroni-and-cheese dinners.

Spaghetti it was. She couldn't offer him any of the other supplies.

She went to her freezer and looked in. One small

container of hamburger meat and a whole chicken sat there.

She'd splurge and add meat to the spaghetti sauce. She pulled the meat out and put it in the frying pan to thaw, wishing again for a microwave.

But she couldn't afford a microwave without a job. Nor would she be able to afford more groceries. That's why her car was so important. Next week's paycheck was supposed to go for groceries.

This week's had to go for rent. She rented on a month-to-month basis, with the understanding that if she dropped over fifteen days behind she'd be evicted. She had three days to go.

Her jobs just weren't bringing in enough money to support her, and she didn't know what she was going to do.

When she'd walked in today and seen her manager's face, she'd realized her parents had found out where she was.

Maggie had asked the manager point-blank if her parents were behind her dismissal. He'd avoided her eyes when he said no.

She had her answer.

She'd fought her parents on the decision about her unborn child, and they were determined that she leave the area…. Her chest tightened on that thought.

She would not think about the confrontation that had forced her from the only home she'd ever known, forced her into working the way she was. Through her trials, though, she'd come to appreciate money. All her life she'd had everything. It was good for her to find out what it was like to have nothing.

Or at least she kept telling herself that.

Deep down inside, though, she felt lonely. God seemed so far away, as if he didn't care. She couldn't understand why He'd let everything happen to her that had.

Seeing that the meat was thawed, she opened a can of tomato sauce and then, thinking that both Tyler and Jake were big men, decided to open two. She'd find a way to buy more groceries.

She'd find a job.

At the thought of a job, she wondered what job Jake had in mind for her. Without references, no one would look at her résumé. If the job was in Baton Rouge, well, she might as well forget about it right now. Her parents controlled a huge business in Baton Rouge and were very well known in the business world. That was why she didn't work there now. They'd put the word out that she was being a problem and rebelling. So of course no one wanted her. And if she did get hired, her parents would hear about it and make sure she didn't keep the job.

She was too much of an embarrassment to them.

Maggie turned abruptly away from the sauce and went to the cabinets, where she pulled out a pan. After filling it with water, she dropped the noodles in to cook.

Looking around, she wondered what Jake would think of where she lived. The trailer had come furnished. A small, checked, broken-down couch sat against one wall; a chair across from it, with a coffee table in between.

She hurried across the room and snatched up her

nightgown, which was lying on the couch. The shag carpet was clean. Though she didn't have a vacuum, she'd used a broom yesterday to sweep it out.

The linoleum in the kitchen was cracked in places but had been mopped.

A small table sat in the corner with two chairs. On it was one place mat and a napkin holder—and a dead bug.

Yuck!

She hated the bugs. She'd never had bugs at her old house. Maggie went over and used a paper towel to sweep it into the garbage. One spray, maybe two more, and the place would be devoid of vermin.

A knock on the door sounded just as an engine started up. Maggie hurried over to answer it.

Jake stood there.

"Where's your friend going?" she asked, seeing the other man driving away.

"He said to tell you thank-you, but he had to get home."

"Oh." She shifted uncomfortably; then, realizing she was keeping him outside, forced down her fears and stepped back. "Come on in."

He nodded, a gentle smile on his face. "Thank you."

He sniffed, and his mouth shifted into a wide grin. "That smells good."

Maggie actually blushed. She was glad she'd gone to the trouble to add meat. "Thank you. It's not much. But I hope you like it."

Jake smiled at her. "I'm sure it will be delicious."

She returned his smile. She couldn't help it. Despite her wariness around men, she liked Jake. He had a warmth about him that she hadn't seen in other men before.

Old bitterness reared its ugly head. After everything that had happened, she had at least expected her church and her family to support her. Yet they hadn't. Not one person had had the guts to stand up with her. Nor had a single person comforted her. Every single one had blamed her for what had happened, believed her a liar, a Jezebel, a Mary Magdalene....

"I'm sorry. Come on in. I have juice, milk and water to drink. I was just about to make up some tea, though."

He smiled. "Tea sounds fine."

"It's herbal," she warned, a hint of defiance creeping into her voice.

He frowned and walked forward. She stiffened, not sure what he was going to say. He floored her when he took her hand and stroked it.

"I'm really sorry about my surprise out there. My only excuse is that I was so captivated by your face I never looked lower."

She burst out laughing. "Now, there's a line I've never heard."

His smile returned, his eyes sparkled. "Be that as it may, I can only beg your forgiveness."

Ruefully Maggie shook her head. "I'll forgive you if you set the table."

She pulled out two plates and silverware and handed them to him.

Jake easily arranged the table, noting the layout with a discerning eye. This woman was low on funds.

He'd been in enough houses before to tell. The cabinets were bare, with nothing hanging on the wall to hint at permanence. And her clothes were probably secondhand since they didn't fit her very well.

He felt guilty eating a meal she had prepared. He wondered if she had enough food. But he wouldn't ask her. Jake didn't know her well enough and wouldn't stick his nose in unless he felt directed by God.

Besides, he still had the idea for a job that might work. But first, he had to put her at ease. He didn't know why she was so worried, unless pastors just made her nervous.

"Have you lived here long?" he asked, taking the hot pot of noodles from her hands and setting it on the table.

"Thank you," she said, and turned back to the stove to finish the sauce. "No. I moved in here two months ago when I came to this area."

He nodded. "Here, let me help you," he said, lifting the pan with the sauce in it from her.

"I'm pregnant, not helpless," she muttered.

He grinned. "Consider it chivalrous. As long as there's someone here to lift for you, why do it yourself?"

"I don't want to turn into a lazy housewife," she returned, sitting down.

He smiled, but his eyes were serious as he said, "I doubt that'd ever happen."

She put her napkin in her lap.

"Do you mind if we pray?" he queried.

Surprised, she lifted her eyes. "Not at all."

He watched her wariness finally fade, and she bowed her head.

After a quick prayer, they served up their plates.

"So, what about this job?" she asked.

Jake felt guilty for keeping her in suspense when he saw how interested she was, though she tried to hide it. "It's here in town."

"Not in Baton Rouge?"

He shook his head. "No. My secretary just quit...."

"Your secretary?"

Jake saw he'd surprised her again. "I guess I didn't explain enough earlier. That's why I inadvertently splashed you. I was talking on the phone and had just found out Shirley quit. I have no replacement and no idea who to hire. I need someone who has good book-keeping skills, as well as secretarial skills. The person would also need to know about lumber and building and things of that nature, if possible. You see, we're undertaking a major building project for the inner-city youth and I'm the one who is spearheading the project."

"What project?" she asked.

"A large recreational center, a place where kids can go and be safe."

She nodded. He could see the cautious hope in her eyes. "I think I could handle the job. But what about references?"

Holding up his fork that had spaghetti on it, he said, "This is reference enough."

"I'm serious," Maggie said, frowning. "I don't

have any references. I can't get any. Why would you consider hiring me without them?''

He wondered if Maggie realized how negative she sounded. Patiently he explained, ''Any woman who is trusting enough to fix a stranger a meal simply because he helped her out is reference enough with me. In my opinion it tells me you aren't totally self-absorbed and that you care.''

She stiffened. ''You've drawn a lot of conclusions from one simple act of kindness.''

''Maybe God is prompting me, too,'' he quipped.

She didn't return his smile. He cleared his throat. ''The hours would be full-time. Of course, with your condition, we could certainly allow time for rests and doctors appointments. And the last person who helped me also ran the children's programs and assisted me on Saturdays with the kids.''

Puzzled, she asked, ''Just what type of job is this? Lumber, kids, children's programs? Do you treat your entire staff this way?''

Jake stilled. He'd told her what his job was, hadn't he? Surely he wouldn't have forgotten something so important that would put the woman at ease immediately and stop her from worrying about him being some rapist. ''Didn't I tell you what I do for a living?'' he asked.

Caution immediately returned, dominating her small round face, and she set her fork down. ''No, you didn't.''

He widened his eyes in dismay. ''I'm so sorry, Maggie. I'd thought I mentioned it when I introduced myself. I'm the local pastor at the church down the road.''

Chapter Three

She paled.

He'd seen it before. People oftentimes reacted negatively to his position. He just hadn't pegged Maggie as that type. Then she glanced down at her stomach, and he saw her problem. "Maggie," he said, pulling her look back to him by the soft yet authoritative tone in his voice. "I'm still the same person I was ten minutes ago. So are you. I still want you for the job."

She glanced everywhere before finally, reluctantly, turning her gaze back to him. "If you're willing to try me out on a trial basis, how can I refuse? What about my car?" she added, pushing her plate away. "Can you tell me if it's working so I can get there?"

"Didn't I mention the house?"

"What house?"

Jake ran a hand through his hair. "You've disrupted more than my dinner, Maggie." He was usually so efficient, keeping his mind on the problem at hand. Maggie had the ability to make him forget everything. "There's a small house next to the church. The rent is very cheap. It's only a two-bedroom, eight hundred square feet. But it's roomy enough for one person. My last secretary lived there."

He named a price that was lower than what she paid here.

Her eyes widened. "You're not misquoting the amount on purpose, are you?"

"No. Since the job doesn't pay much above minimum wage, the rent is cut way back. We make just enough to keep up repairs and pay the taxes each year. That way, the secretary, who ends up spending almost as much time as I do at church, will have a place to live that doesn't cost an arm and a leg."

"Where do you live?"

He could tell she hadn't meant to blurt that out. She actually blushed. He couldn't help but grin. "Well, I don't live there," he drawled, and her blush deepened. "The house is yours, if you want it. If not, we'll rent it out to someone else."

How could she pass it up? "I guess I agree," she replied. Staring at the man in front of her, she still found it hard to believe he was a pastor. He was so good-looking and so sweet. He hadn't condemned her for her condition or questioned her about it. Instead, compassion showed in his eyes as he smiled at her. Not pity. Never pity. She would have thrown him out if he'd given her the look of others. That look of condemnation. The look her parents had given her. No, he simply smiled at her as if she was an actual person, as if he might understand what she was going through.

Of course, that was impossible. Why would he have to worry about what everyone thought of him or be on guard constantly?

Then she realized that was it. As a pastor, she imagined many people had the opportunity to dissect him over lunch, just as her parents had done with their own pastor. Maybe he did know something of the humiliation and pain she'd been through because of the way everyone had treated her.

Still, working for a pastor. At a church. She wasn't sure. She loved God. But she hurt so much. It seemed that everything that could go wrong had gone wrong in the past seven months. And it all evolved around her family and church friends.

She'd blamed God for casting her out.

I will never leave you or forsake you.

That inner voice reminded her of God's promise. Then why? Why had all this happened to her? Why wasn't she allowed to have any happiness?

Jake was offering her a chance at peace, if not happiness. And she had just said she would take it. "I'll be glad to move in then," she said, and that settled that.

"Good!" He clapped his hands, finished off his spaghetti, then stood. "I need to get going. Listen, is two days from now too soon to move you? That would be Saturday, and I'm sure I can find some men to come over and pack up whatever you want to take. We could get you moved in and unpacked in one day."

"I don't have much. The furniture's not mine. All I have is one suitcase, maybe two."

He paused, his look probing her. She stiffened, certain the questions would come. Instead, he smiled. "Great. Then we'll have the house ready for you Saturday. I'll come by with a couple of the women so we can help you get the house cleaned up for inspection."

"I don't need any help."

Jake rolled his eyes. "Don't balk, Maggie. Of course you need help. You're pregnant."

"I haven't had any help yet," she blurted out, then gasped; Maggie clapped a hand over her mouth.

Silence fell, and Jake studied her a minute. He reached out and stroked her cheek with his finger. "You've had a tough time of it, haven't you, Maggie? And it's hard for you to trust."

Unexpected tears filled her eyes.

He dropped his hand and cleared his throat, stepping back instead of forward the way he wanted to. "Don't worry. You'll be welcome at church."

"But what will people say to you?" she asked, not believing him. "You're going to catch the very devil for hiring a single pregnant woman."

There, she'd said it. She was single and not married. She couldn't tell him the rest. But that was enough to condemn her in most people's eyes.

She waited. A slow smile curved his lips, lighting up his face. "'Be joyful in hope, patient in affliction, faithful in prayer,'" he quoted from Romans.

"And what do you mean by that?" she asked, not understanding.

He grinned. "Well," he drawled, "we can *hope* no one says anything. But if someone does, then we can be patient and pray and allow God to handle the problem."

She shook her head. "An optimist."

"God gave us hope when He sent His son, Maggie. Why let someone's possible actions rob us of that?"

Maggie raised weary eyes to Jake's. "I've learned already that the world isn't a place of optimism."

"Look inside yourself. Ask God to restore your joy. Don't let them," he said, waving his hand toward the outside, "rob you of it. There are always going to be negative people around who can't stand to see you succeed or be happy. And there are always going to be people to kick you while you're down. But if I think you're a good secretary, as I know you're a good person, then no one is going to tell me who to hire and who to fire."

"But you don't know if I'm a good secretary," she argued, frustrated.

He grinned. "Then don't disappoint me."

He went to the door. Pausing on the bottom step, he turned back toward her. "See you Saturday, Maggie-May," he singsonged.

She couldn't help the reluctant smile that came to her lips.

She'd never met anyone like Jake.

Not even her ex-fiancé.

Her ex-fiancé. Boy, had that been a mistake. She'd thought he loved her. She'd thought she loved him. But then she'd changed her mind.

She didn't want to think about the trouble, think

about the nightmares it gave her. Instead, she wanted to think about the laughing eyes of the gorgeous man who had just given her a ride home and rescued her from certain poverty.

But she knew better than to think it was only Jake who had rescued her. "Thank you, God, for providing a way when I couldn't see one. I'm glad about this job. But—" she walked over to the couch and sank onto it "—I don't know if I can believe in happily ever after again. Every time I think I've finally found a job, or a place to live, or something great, it seems the rug is jerked out from under me. Is this going to be any different?"

She got up and went into the kitchen. She could save the spaghetti and have enough to last until Saturday. Then maybe she could make her groceries last until her next paycheck.

And maybe, just maybe, she'd pass Jake's approval and get to stay at this job longer than a month or two.

Chapter Four

"You didn't tell me you lived right behind me!"

Jake, who had just finished the inner-city work an hour earlier before swinging by to pick up Maggie, smiled, surprised. "Does it matter?"

Maggie frowned warily. "I can only imagine the talk there will be."

"You're my secretary, Maggie. My last secretary lived here. The entire church knows it. Don't worry about it."

Maggie still didn't appear convinced. Jake wondered what drove her to be so cautious but didn't ask. "As you can see," he said, going on into the house, "here is the living room. The carpet is old but clean. The couch actually folds out into an extra bed if you have company." Jake wondered if she minded an orange couch and chair. "Shirley had them reupholstered in those colors. You might, uh, try throwing a small blanket across the back."

Jake heard a chuckle behind him and turned. "Yellow and orange are fine. And yes, I have a small blanket to cut the glare."

Relieved, Jake smiled. "I never asked her what color she wanted to redo the material in. At least the curtains aren't white."

Jake pointed at the light-blue curtains until he saw Maggie's wince.

"Let's just see the rest of the house, shall we?"

Jake nodded. Glancing around the room, he suddenly realized that Shirley must have had very poor taste in decorating. Blue curtains, tan rug, orange and yellow furniture.

"The kitchen has a small table for four in it. The stove is gas and there's a frost-free refrigerator."

Maggie thought it was much nicer than the trailer she'd been in. The living room might be a bit bright, but this room, she thought, with the light white-and-blue floor with soft blue-and-pink wallpaper, was homey.

"One of the women repapered the walls before you moved in."

"That explains the smell. I wondered what that smell was." The counters were clean, and there was even a toaster and a food processor on the counter.

"To the back are the two bedrooms and the bathroom."

Maggie strode there to look. The master bedroom was bigger than the trailer she'd been in, with a double bed and two chests and a small vanity. She turned to the bathroom. It was old but very neat. "I don't think I've ever seen a claw-foot tub before."

"That's next on our list of renovations. This house is more than fifty years old. We've been renovating one room at a time over the past year. The kitchen and the second bedroom are done."

Maggie went to the second bedroom and smiled. "Earthtones, yellows and greens. It's beautiful."

Maggie heard Jake's step approaching and turned, feeling trapped in the hall. Thankfully, Jake stopped near the entrance. "Of course we'll be glad to remove the bed and put in a crib for you. Tyler would have gotten that done earlier—"

"Oh, no, Mr.—uh, Reverend, Pastor..." Helplessly, she lifted her hands. She could feel the blush warming her cheeks.

"Just 'Jake.'"

His warm smile could melt chocolate on a winter day. It certainly melted her heart. She found herself smiling back. "Well then, just Jake," she said, "please don't bother with that until I know what I'm going to do. Or if you're certain you even want me here."

Jake's smile left his face. The shimmer in his dark eyes dimmed. "Maggie, I don't know why you're so worried, but I think you should know, we're a small church. If you can type and have any kind of head for business we can work the rest out. Unless you aren't happy here, then there might be a problem. So please, stop worrying."

Maggie nodded. "I'm sorry." She didn't say she'd had so many jobs in the past six months that she'd become cynical. Or that she was certain it was only a matter of time before her parents found out where she was. They would exert some sort of nasty little influence to get her out of the area so she wouldn't be an embarrassment to them. Again.

Seeing Jake's concerned expression, she pasted the smile back on her face. "This is more than I could hope for. Why don't you show me where I am going to work."

Jake nodded, relieved, though still concerned that she was hiding more than she was telling. *Father, help her,* he silently asked. "Right this way. As I said, the church has only between 100 and 150 in attendance, according to what is going on. Our average crowd is just over 100. Of course, we have the day care, which has 185 children, grades kindergarten through third. I never dreamed it would grow so fast."

Jake led her across a small path lined with azaleas to the church. The smell emanating from the pink and purple blooms was sweet, teasing her nostrils and surrounding her in a soft gentle fragrance that relaxed her.

"I love azaleas," Maggie murmured.

Jake smiled. "Mrs. Titterson wanted to donate them to the church. She thought they'd be beautiful lining the path here as well as both yards." Jake motioned back at the houses. "They are beautiful in the spring. We have crepe myrtles in the front of the church and snowball bushes along the far side. You'll notice the bridal bushes around the parking lot."

"I never met a man who knew so much about shrubbery." Maggie glanced at him curiously.

Jake turned and grinned at her. "Didn't you realize

a pastor is a jack-of-all-trades? Who do you think helped plant all these bushes?''

Maggie chuckled. Jake liked the way it sounded, low, warm, husky. Realizing where his thoughts had drifted, he stopped, disconcerted. Shaking himself mentally, he stepped off the path and in front of the long rectangular concrete building.

"This was once a business. We bought it, then tore out the inside and rebuilt it. It was big enough for anything we might want to do later. I'm thankful now that we did that. Otherwise we wouldn't have been able to start up a school."

Maggie nodded.

Jake decided she probably wasn't interested and held open the door. He saw her look down at the carpet. "The blue doesn't show dirt as easily. It was a choice between that and red. If you'll just turn to the right, you'll find the offices. The left leads out to the sanctuary and the school, which I'll be glad to show you later."

Jake reached out and took Maggie's elbow in his hand to guide her down the hall. He'd thought to do it as a gentlemanly gesture but found he liked the feel of her soft skin in his hand. He immediately released it. This woman was a walking problem. He had no doubt she would flee if she knew his thoughts ran toward the curious and I find you fascinating.

He didn't understand it. He hadn't known her long enough to be attracted to her. Besides, she was pregnant. There was a broken heart in there somewhere. And though he felt she was the right one for the job, saw a softness in her, that didn't tell him one iota about her relationship with God.

No, indeed, he had no right to be wondering if Maggie was married, divorced, single or carrying twins or quadruplets for that matter.

Besides, he'd learned long ago that women didn't fall for men who owned nothing. Jake had a salary, and a roof over his head, but there wasn't much left over. He had been saving what he could. Soon he would be able to buy a new car since the other one had over 100,000 miles. Janie had made it clear that if he wouldn't go to a bigger church where he could make better money, she didn't want him.

He remembered that breakup just before he'd moved to this church. Jake had never completely recovered. Janie couldn't understand why he didn't want a better job. When he'd tried to explain that this church was where God wanted him, that his heart was in building a place for the inner-city youth, she'd broken off their engagement.

Jake had decided then and there to concentrate fully on his ministry. God called him to do a job, and he would do that job. If love came one day, fine. But he wasn't going to search for it.

"Here we are," he said to Maggie.

Glancing around the office, he tried to imagine what she saw. "It's rather messy right now. I've been trying to do the filing, and Jennifer Dalton has been coming in to help."

"Jennifer?" Maggie asked, still studying the office.

Jake nodded. He moved over to the desk, gathered four file folders and straightened them. "She's the head of our day-care center now. A wonderful woman. You'll love her.''

He put the folders in the box on her desk and then smiled. "This will be your desk. The copier is here." He pointed to the corner. "And we have the latest in word processing on the computer. My office is through the door behind me. Since I do a lot of counseling, I need privacy, so you'll have to screen my calls and run interference. Most everyone here is really understanding. There are a few, though..." He trailed off and shrugged. "You know how that goes. Life isn't perfect."

Maggie nodded. She looked around again and then toward the door.

Jake took her out and showed her the day care and the rest of the church.

"Jennifer!"

Maggie noted how Jake's face suddenly lit up with a bright smile for the young girl coming their way. She was petite, the girl-next-door type, with long blond hair falling out of a French braid that was pinned up on the back of her head. She wore a purple and gold LSU shirt and baggy jeans. As she approached, Maggie realized there was paint all over her clothes and on her hands.

"This must be Maggie," the young woman said, coming forward, beaming.

On closer inspection, Maggie realized Jennifer was older than she looked. Small smile lines around her eyes gave that away. Maggie smiled and nodded. "And you're the famed Jennifer I've heard so much about."

She actually blushed. "Jake has been telling tales again? Don't you listen to a one of them." Turning on Jake, the young woman gave him a reproving look. "You didn't tell her about the snake, did you? Or the rappelling accident?"

Jake lifted his hands in surrender. "I haven't told her anything except what an excellent job you do here."

Maggie liked the way the light jacket stretched on Jake's shoulders, outlining them, showing their width. She'd never seen a pastor who wore jeans with a jacket. But it suited him.

"Oh," Jennifer said.

Maggie glanced at Jennifer and saw she was pink again. Then what she had said registered. "Rappelling accident?"

Jennifer turned even brighter red. "Don't ask. Maybe one day we'll have time to sit down, and I can tell you all about it. Unfortunately, I was just about to go wash up. Gage is coming by and picking me up for lunch, and I got carried away with the kids and didn't realize it was so late."

Jake shook his head. "I'm just showing Maggie around. Go on."

"Nice meeting you," Jennifer said.

Maggie murmured her agreement. "Rappelling accident?" she asked when Jennifer was gone.

Jake chuckled and led her back toward the front entrance of the church. "It's a long story. But it ends well. Jennifer got a pet snake out of it, and a husband."

"You're kidding."

Jake shook his head. "Gage is quite a man. Come on, let's go out this door and get your stuff unpacked from the car. Then I'll let you rest."

Jake pushed open the door for her and Maggie went out. She had thought Jake unusual in how friendly and outgoing he was. She had never met a pastor quite like him.

He'd been enthusiastic, fun loving, excited, when he had picked her up and then rattled on and on about the kids and the puppet show. While showing her the house, he had actually been nervous about whether she was going to like it. But the house was a deal she couldn't pass up. Who cared about the yellow-and-orange furniture or the yellow-and-orange coat rack in the corner?

Maggie had heard the pride as he had talked about helping plant the bushes, and the joy behind his words as he'd talked about the people at the church.

There had been no formality or reserve in his voice or his stance. His fluid movements as he'd taken her around proved to her how at ease he was with this.

"Meeeooowwr."

Maggie didn't even see the pitiful sight until she was almost upon it. "Oh, my heavens!"

Maggie stared in horror at the bloody mess that was a peach-colored cat. At least she thought it was peach. It was hard to tell with all the blood. "Jake!"

Jake moved up by Maggie and put a hand on her shoulder. "Let me handle it, Maggie."

Jake started forward, and the cat hissed. He paused. "Maybe we'd better call animal control. The poor thing looks to be in bad shape."

The cat lay there on its side, breathing hard, fur ripped away in tufts. She thought it had been in a cat fight since part of an ear was missing, except that she'd never seen a cat break another cat's tail. And that had to be one of the problems with this cat, since its tail lay at such an odd angle. One leg was twisted, too. Tears came to Maggie's eyes. "We can't just leave it here."

"I know, I know. Let me go call city hall and see if they can send someone out. I'll be right back."

Jake hurried in to call for help. Maggie continued to stare at the cat. Silent tears fell as she watched it labor for breath. She could see the terror and pain in its eyes and felt it reach out to her and wrap itself around her heart. It hadn't been too many months ago she'd felt pain and terror.

Please don't let it die, God. Please, please, please, she prayed, and inched forward.

The cat hissed again, and she whimpered. "Please don't let it bite me. Please, please, please."

It hissed once more and then made an awful, plaintive sound. "Father, help it. Help me. I'm not letting it be die just because it's in pain and scared."

The cat eyed every inch she moved.

Maggie got close enough to kneel down. She put her hand out, and the cat swiped at it with one of its uninjured paws. Maggie jumped but didn't back away. "I'm not going to hurt you. Please let me help you, sweetie. Just let me help you. No one helped me, but I can help you," she whispered.

Carefully she moved her hand closer.

This time the cat only eyed her hand.

She slipped it under the cat's head, then its body. The cat growled.

Maggie made sympathetic noises, crying right along with the cat as she slipped her other hand under it and then picked it up.

Its tail hung sideways. "Oh dear—oh dear," she cried, over and over until she had gathered the cat to her bosom. "We'll get you help immediately. I promise you. I won't let you down."

Maggie heard the church door open. "The animal shelter...Maggie!" Alarm in his voice tensed her spine.

Jake hurried forward when he saw the bloody mess in her arms. "You're pregnant. What if it has rabies? What if it had bitten you?"

Maggie's face turned as hard as stone. "Will you drive me to a vet?"

Jake hesitated then nodded. "Just let me take—"

The cat hissed and swiped at Jake. His eyes widened and he lifted his hands in surrender, backing up.

"Okay. Okay. You hold it. But I'll be praying the thing doesn't take its pain out on you before we get to the vet."

"It won't," Maggie said, looking back down at the cat.

Jake paused in pulling his keys from his jeans pocket. He eyed her his features probing, searching before he nodded, "You know, Maggie-May, I think you just might be right."

He slipped a hand to her lower back, then guided her toward the truck. "There's a clinic less than two blocks away."

Chapter Five

She wouldn't let them cut its tail off.

Jake was still shaking his head over that. Jake sneezed again as he turned into the driveway next to the church.

"Are you sure you're not allergic to cats?" Maggie asked worriedly.

Jake shook his head. "I'm not allergic to anything." He rubbed at his watering eyes. "Just dust or something, I'm sure."

He pulled to a stop and hopped out, then went around the hood to open her door. Once again the cat hissed at him.

He sneezed.

"Be careful," she warned when he reached out to ease her out of the truck's seat. "I don't want you to scare her."

Scare her? Jake looked at the way the cat rolled its eyes at him and didn't think the animal was in any way scared. "Careful, now. We don't want you falling."

"I'm fine," Maggie said, holding the cat close. "I still can't believe she only had a cut on her side, was missing part of her ear and had a broken tail and broken foot."

"Well, if the doc was right and it climbed up in someone's car, I'd say it was real lucky."

Maggie nodded, sighing when both feet found solid ground. "The cat is a she, not an it."

"Oh." Jake nodded. He went ahead of her and opened the door to her house. As she approached he sneezed again. "You sure you'll be okay with her here? Doc offered to keep her for you until the owner was found."

Maggie shook her head. "I'll look after her. We don't even know if she had an owner. There were no records. That's why the vet went ahead and gave her shots."

Jake sighed. He watched Maggie cooing to the cat the entire time the cat growled back at her. The hair on the back of his neck stood up at how mean that cat sounded, but Maggie sat there and made faces at the animal.

"If you need anything…"

Maggie looked up, opened her mouth, then shook her head.

"What?"

"Nothing. I can get it later."

Jake studied her as she went over and sat down on the couch. His gaze drifted to the cat. Suddenly it dawned on him. "Cat food."

Maggie glanced up, surprised. "Yes. I do need cat food. But I am paying for this."

She narrowed her eyes to let him know she was serious.

Jake shrugged. "I didn't mind paying for the vet. You saved the cat when the shelter would have put her down. It was the least I could do."

Maggie laid the cat carefully on her jacket, which was on the couch, and stood. She crossed the room to her purse and opened it. Jake watched her discreetly count out her money, then hand him some. "I would appreciate it. I'm just afraid to leave her right now."

Jake smiled. "No problem. I'll run up to the store and be right back."

Maggie's face softened. "Thank you."

Her smile could easily knock a man off his feet. He couldn't remember anyone with a smile like that. He found himself grinning like an idiot. "Uh, yeah." Jake cleared his throat. "Okay. I'll just…go."

Maggie nodded, turning back to the cat when she growled again.

Jake shook his head and left, sneezing three times before he got out the door. He tried to remember if he'd ever been around cats and couldn't recall a single incident except when he was a child. "No. I do not have allergies," he reassured himself.

Jake turned and headed across the driveway to his truck. He saw Jennifer and her husband locking up the day care for the evening and paused.

Jennifer and Gage came over. Gage stuck out his

hand and Jake automatically shook it. "How's the new secretary? She getting settled in?"

Jake nodded, blinking at the itchy sensation. "She's fine. I'm sorry, Jennifer, that I was gone so long. It took the doc longer to patch up that cat than we realized."

"No problem." Jennifer peered at him. "Cat allergies?" she asked sympathetically.

"No." Jake shook his head. "I just...the truck needs to be cleaned out bad."

Gage raised an eyebrow in disbelief.

Jennifer looked confused. "If you say so. Do you need anything before I leave?"

Again Jake shook his head. "I'm on my way to the store. No one called, did they?"

"Yes. Mrs. Rawley. She wanted to make sure this was her Sunday to work in the nursery. Gloria called and rescheduled her appointment from Monday to Tuesday to talk with you. She said she just couldn't make it."

Jake sighed. Gloria was putting off their talk and that worried him. She had come to him about the problems going on in her marriage and their one talk was enough to make him really concerned.

"And Sister Hollings called. She wanted to talk to you about the music again. She says it's way too loud on Sunday morning. If it wasn't turned down, then she said she was going to turn it down herself."

Jake smiled. "I know...that guitar..."

"Just drives me crazy," Jennifer said with him, and they both chuckled.

"Gotta love her," he said. "You left the messages on my desk?"

"Yeah. They're all there except Gloria's. I slipped that in your top desk drawer on top of the phone book."

"Thank you, Jennifer. I'll see you tomorrow."

"You get some sleep tonight," Gage said, slipping his arm around his wife but keeping his gaze on Jake. "Those plans for the inner-city program can wait until later."

Jake groaned. "I completely forgot."

Jennifer elbowed her husband. "Thanks, Gage."

Gage shrugged. "Sorry."

"Seriously, Jake. I've looked over them and talked with the committee. They've agreed to give you another week."

Wearily Jake nodded. "Fine. Fine. Good night."

They waved and left.

Jake climbed in his truck and ran up to the local dollar store.

Once there, Jake went through the aisles, trying to decide what the cat would need and if he could pay for it with the money Maggie had given him.

He shook his head.

Impossible.

With God, all things are possible, he acknowledged silently. "So, how are we going to work this out so as not to embarrass her?" he muttered.

Jake thought.

They could afford cat food. That was a must. Cat litter, too. But that left only three dollars for a litter box and bowls.

Remembering being on the streets when he was a kid, he smiled. Other people had had pets, but they certainly hadn't been able to afford all the fancy stuff advertised on these aisles as musts for cat owners. No, a simple bowl out of the kitchen and a plastic-lined box had suited them fine.

He took the two items up the cash register and paid for them, feeling guilty. Of course, what Maggie didn't know was that he'd had the cabinets filled from their food pantry as a welcome gift from the church. So maybe this money wouldn't be missed so much when she realized she had food.

After paying for the items, he took them out to the truck and hurried back to Maggie's.

He knocked.

"Come in, Jake."

He opened the door and went inside, carrying the items. "You really should have that locked."

He stopped, unable to believe what he was seeing. Maggie had taken the extra pillow, put her raincoat over it, then a sheet and finally the cat on top of it.

The cat saw him and growled.

He sneezed.

Maggie looked up, noticed the bag and smiled. "Thank you."

Jake handed her the food. "I'll carry the litter. It's too heavy."

"Okay." Maggie nodded and went into the kitchen. She rummaged around until she found two old bowls, then filled one with water and one with food.

"About the door..." he began.

''I would have had it locked, but I went out to get my suitcases. I had just gotten back in before you arrived.''

''I told you I'd get those for you,'' Jake said, somehow feeling he'd failed to help her.

Maggie glanced over her shoulder at him. Jake noted the way her hair had come out of the ponytail and several strands fell loosely against her cheek. ''That wasn't necessary, Jake.''

Jake stared at her smile, thinking how soft it made her look. When she tipped her head quizzically he cleared his throat. ''Oh, um…well, carrying those can't be good for you as far along as you are.''

Maggie chuckled, finished pouring the food and brought both bowls back over to the cat. ''There you go, my darlin','' she crooned, obviously not hearing the growl when she rubbed the cat on the head.

''I'm just over seven months pregnant, Jake. I have eight weeks to go. Actually, tomorrow I'll be seven months. Anyway, I'm big but not helpless. The doctor at the clinic told me I'd get a lot bigger the last two months.''

Jake nodded. ''Elizabeth was as big as a barrel before her twins were born.''

Maggie laughed. ''I hope I don't look like a barrel.''

Jake flushed. ''I didn't mean that.''

Maggie looked up impishly. ''You're a pastor. I thought all pastors had a talent to wax eloquent.''

Her attitude surprised a laugh out of him. ''I don't know where my talent for words has gone. I have never been able to wax eloquent, Maggie-May. I'm just a country boy at heart and I'm afraid that comes out in my sermons.''

Maggie didn't answer but slowly pushed herself to her feet.

Jake couldn't resist the urge to reach out to her. He caught her elbow to steady her, wondering how she kept her balance.

She must have known anyway what he thought because of the knowing smile she gave him. ''Thank you, Jake, for helping me today.''

Jake nodded, taking that as his cue to leave. He started toward the door.

''And thank you for the food in the cabinets.''

So, she knew about that. ''That was a welcoming gift from the church. We have a food pantry, and it's well stocked right now.''

Maggie had an unfathomable look on her face. Jake hoped he hadn't gone too far. He waited as she studied him. Finally, she nodded. ''It means a lot.''

Relieved, Jake smiled. ''Good. You're part of our family now, Maggie. You shouldn't go in need of food or help. If you have a need, please tell someone.''

''I haven't even attended your church yet, Jake. How can I be part of your family?''

Jake saw the yearning in her eyes and wondered at it. Was it loneliness? A desire to belong somewhere? He didn't know, but he wanted to reassure her. ''Whether you attended our church or another, we're all family. As a Christian, that's what God expects. But I've met you, you're working for me, I know you as part of God's family. So, we're here for you.''

Maggie slowly shook her head, the light dimming in her eyes. "I've heard that preached, Jake, but I have yet to see that truly practiced."

Jake wanted to retort that she'd been going to the wrong churches. But he didn't. He couldn't judge what he didn't know, where he hadn't been. And he was glad it wasn't his job. Instead, he said, "Give us a try. I'm not saying we're perfect. I don't think there's a church that is, but God won't fail you when we do."

Maggie thought about what he said and nodded. God hadn't failed her. She didn't understand how this had happened to her, why she'd ended up pregnant, but she did know that every time she had lost a job, something had turned up almost immediately. She had never run out of food, though she had come close. And when she had been at her lowest, this man had appeared, offering her hope again—or at least it looked that way. She'd have to reserve judgment on that until later.

"No, God never fails us, does He?" she repeated softly, her heart echoing loudly in her own ears. "Thank you, Jake."

Jake nodded. "Well, let me get out of here so you can get some sleep. Church starts at ten in the morning. I hope to see you there."

Maggie nodded again. "Good night."

"Good night."

Jake went out the door but paused. "Lock it before I leave the porch."

Maggie held back a chuckle. She walked across the floor and locked the door.

She heard his feet echo on the steps and then peeked out the window. He walked—no, it reminded her more of a stroll—to his car as if he had all the time in the world, as if there weren't any problems pressing down on his shoulders, as if he were happy and carefree. "Oh, Father, why can't I feel like that? Where has my joy gone? Have I been down in the pit so long that I can't see out?"

Maggie turned and headed back over to the cat, which was trying to lap up the water. "You poor thing," she whispered, and bent down to help her.

The cat let out a whimper, then allowed her to help. "You don't fool me. As much as you're hurting and you act like you don't want the help, deep down you do. Maybe you don't realize it yet, but I'm not going to let you sit here and die of thirst when I can help you."

A line of a song came to her: "He's my rock, He's my fortress, He's my deliverer...."

"Father, You've been my rock, or I would have never made it this far. My fortress. I don't know that I've allowed You to be that, hiding myself away. And my deliverer..."

Maggie sighed. "Please, Father, be my deliverer. Deliver me from the fear of the night, the fear of being alone...and the fear of sleeping. Jake was right. You never fail. If we would only turn to You immediately, instead of hiding away, we'd be so much better off."

Maggie felt a peace. She noted the cat had stopped drinking, having gained her fill. Maggie moved the bowl back and stood, then went to fix a box for the litter. She hadn't thought of litter; she was glad Jake had.

"Thank You, Father for sending this man my way. Help me to learn to trust him. And keep any disasters from befalling him because of our relationship."

She finished the box, set it next to the cat and vowed to keep an ear open in case the cat had any problems in the night.

Maggie went to her room, changed into her orange nightgown and crawled into bed. For the first time in a long time, she felt, if not total peace, then a safety knowing there was someone nearby if she needed help.

The dancing brown eyes of Jake Mathison stayed before her face as she drifted off to sleep, thinking maybe things might not be so bad after all.

Chapter Six

Maggie had heard the old saying "Don't count your chickens before they are hatched." And after all she'd been through the past six months, she should have learned that lesson.

Jake was a nice man. He seemed like a jewel after what she'd experienced. But just because he said everything would be okay didn't mean that it would.

Oh, Maggie thought it had gone fine this morning when she'd gotten up and dressed in her nicest pants and top that fit over her tummy.

She'd walked over to church and immediately met Gage and Jennifer, who had then introduced her to Max and Kaitland, who had a newborn in her arms and two twins hanging on her legs. Kaitland—or "Katie" as Max had called her—then took her and introduced her to her brother-in-law, Rand, and his wife Elizabeth, who had a small child in her arms.

And on and on it went, until the names had blurred

together. She had been pulled into the midst of these people she had read so much about in the paper.

Maggie had reveled in it. She enjoyed the warmth and joking among them before church and the worship service. This wasn't like her old church. They were freer in the way they worshipped, had all kinds of instruments and really seemed to enjoy church, unlike her parents, who saw it as an imposition.

And then Jake had stood up to preach. He looked wonderful in his nice pair of slacks and casual blazer.

And his preaching was different from what she had heard before. It was…powerful. Not condemning, not filled with dire predictions, but filled with love and hope and promise. Oh, he did touch on the negative issues, but those issues always ended with hope. That hope was Jesus Christ.

She liked Jake's message. It touched her heart unlike any message she had heard in a long time. And she found tears running down her face as she listened. He said that no matter what your circumstances, Jesus was the answer. He had all the answers. He loved and cared and provided, maybe not in the way people expected but in His own way.

Her heart filled with joy at Jake's words as she realized that God would take care of the problems.

At the end, they had an altar call and then church was over.

When people turned to one another and began discussing dinner plans and meetings, Maggie decided to ease her way out.

She needed to check on her cat—Kathryn, as she had named her. Maggie was also starving. For some reason, going for more than two hours without food almost killed her. She would get the shakes and feel that she was actually getting ill.

She saw Jake looking her way and waved slightly, then turned toward the door.

"You're the new secretary?"

Maggie turned, wanting to see who had said that.

Her heart fell to her shoes when she saw the woman. She reminded Maggie of her mother. Proud, haughty and looking down her nose while smiling oh, so sweetly.

"Yes, I am."

"Oh, well. I thought the new secretary was single."

Maggie felt a dull flush rising on her cheeks. Her stomach churned and her hands shook. "I am single. My name is Maggie." Maggie stuck out her hand, just trying to get through this.

The woman took her hand politely. She didn't once glance at Maggie's abdomen, which made it even worse. Maggie knew what the woman was thinking.

"I'm sorry, are you widowed, then, or divorced? I know how hard it can be on a woman in that position. I'm widowed."

The woman said the words, but Maggie could tell she had already been tried and condemned. The woman's eyes were filled with condemnation, even though she smiled.

"No, Mrs., er…"

"Robertson."

"No, Mrs. Robertson, I'm not widowed or divorced, just plain single."

Maggie refused to say another word. If the woman wanted to know how she could be single *and* pregnant, she'd be more than glad to give her an earful. She knew better though.

This woman would spread rumors and innuendo, instead of attacking her, and Jake would be hurt and embarrassed, and then he'd have to ask her to leave....

"I see you've met Mrs. Robertson."

The vibrations of Jake's deep voice ran down her spine, soothing her. His hand touching her back lightly reassured her as nothing else could. "Yes, I have. And so many others I can't even begin to put names and faces to them."

"I hate to interrupt, Mrs. Robertson, but Rand and Max asked me to drag her back over there. They wanted to invite her over for lunch. Excuse us, please."

Mrs. Robertson nodded.

Jake guided Maggie away before Mrs. Robertson could utter a word. She could feel Jake's stare but refused to meet his gaze.

"Remember how I said no church was perfect, Maggie?"

She heard his whisper and nodded, lips tight with worry.

"The woman can be a dear, but she also has a small problem about being judgmental, too. We're praying about it. Ignore her and leave her to me."

"She'll cause problems. She wanted to know about the baby. She found every way she could to ask if the baby was illegitimate, narrowing the options down one by one until there were no others."

"Maggie, that's between you and God. Don't answer anyone's questions if you don't want to. And like I said, leave Mrs. Robertson to me. I spiked her guns when I told her Max and Rand wanted to invite you to dinner. She really likes to be invited over there with the other church members and would never say anything if it would risk her chances of getting an invitation."

"Oh, Jake, that's awful," Maggie said, horrified and just a little proud of his ingenious way of handling it. Tension quickly drained out of her, and she realized her past hurts were coloring her perceptions again.

"Hey, I'm not lying. They do want you to come over for dinner. And they did ask me to come over and grab you. They've seen Mrs. Robertson eat others alive, and wanted you rescued, by the way. I don't know, Maggie. It looks like some of our members have taken a shining to you."

Maggie blushed at Jake's words. Still, she couldn't help but add, "We'll see what happens when everyone figures out I'm not married."

Jake shrugged. "Stop being so hard on yourself. Mrs. Robertson will get over it as she comes to know you. She really is a softy at heart—eventually."

Maggie chuckled. "I'll bet."

"And so are Elizabeth and Kaitland and their husbands. Now, let's go over and—"

"Oh, no, Jake. I can't."

Jake paused and looked down at her. "Are you sure? We've both been invited. I thought you'd love to come, get to meet some of the people from here, maybe make some new friends.''

How could she tell him that crowds bothered her, that she preferred to be alone. ''I have to check on Kathryn, the cat. I named her,'' she said at his quizzical look. '''Captain Kat,''' she said, grinning to hide her nervousness. ''Anyway, I need to check on her and I'm tired. I'm going to rest after that.''

Jake studied her seriously. ''Okay, Maggie-May. But let me tell you something, hiding out isn't going to help the pain go away.''

''Pain?'' Maggie's heart tripped as she thought that he might have some idea what she was going through.

''It's in your eyes when you don't realize anyone is looking. I'm not asking what it is. If you decide you want to tell me, I'm here. Both as a pastor and, I hope, as a friend. It's your choice. But, Maggie, just know there are people here who will care, who will be here if you reach out, okay?''

Maggie nodded, feeling an odd sting in her eyes and nose, and knew she was about to cry. ''Please, make my excuses.''

Jake nodded. ''Okay. I'll see you tonight?''

''Yes,'' she whispered, and hurried toward the back door.

''What happened?''

Jake heard Elizabeth's voice and turned, smiling. ''She's tired and wanted to go home and rest.''

Elizabeth frowned. ''I think she needs a friend.''

Jake sighed. ''Maybe. Give it time, though.''

And he vowed to give Maggie until exactly six

o'clock tonight to get over it before he put his nose in where it probably didn't belong.

"And a trip to the park with ice cream is in my job description?" Maggie smiled, amused, staring at the double scoop of chunky-choco chocolate ice cream that Jake had ordered her. She reached out and took it.

"Yes, it is. The mall closes in an hour, but I wanted you to see something here."

"You keep saying that," Maggie complained good-naturedly, wondering what in the world could be at the park this late at night.

"Like I explained earlier tonight at church, it has to do with the Saturday ministry. You'll be involved in it, so you should have some idea how it works."

"And I'll find out all about that here? At the park? I'll admit this is a place I haven't been to in months, but I don't remember any churches or anything stashed away in some corner somewhere."

Jake shook his head, motioned to her ice cream, then took a lick of his own.

Maggie sighed and tasted hers, and was surprised at how delicious it was. "Oh, my, I'd forgotten how rich their ice cream is here," she murmured, closing her eyes and taking another taste.

She smiled, allowing the ice cream to melt in her mouth before swallowing. When she opened her eyes, Jake was staring at her oddly. "What?" she asked.

"How long has it been since you've had ice cream?"

Maggie flushed and started walking. "I don't get out much."

"I try to come here at least once a month. If I don't I'm sure I'm having withdrawal. Sometimes I even buy a quart and bring it home."

Maggie looked over at Jake, relieved to see him eating his cone and no longer staring as he walked beside her.

She took another bite of her own dessert, relaxing. "So, what brings us here?"

Maggie lifted her cone to lick at it and paused. "Oh, look, a clown." A man dressed in a bright polka-dot clown suit with purple-and-orange hair and a big red nose, sat in the middle of the children's area that this park had for kids to watch special shows.

He was performing tricks and talking to the kids the entire time. What was so amazing to Maggie was that the kids didn't move. Not one twitched.

"This is like your heart," the clown was saying, and held up a dirty handkerchief. "Sometimes we lie, or maybe do something else bad like steal...."

She watched him tucking the hankie in a small rectangular box.

"But Jesus tells us he'll clean our heart, take away the bad and give us a new heart. Just as that hankie was dirty, our hearts get dirty."

He held up the box, showing the kids as they asked how they got new hearts and on and on.

Finally, when they quieted, he held up the box again and smiled. "Oh, it's real simple. You just tell Jesus you're sorry and you want him to help you and your heart will be made all clean. Remember the hankie? Well, we don't have to do the washing or the scrubbing—God does that.'' He opened the box back up and pulled out the hankie, and to Maggie's amazement, it was white, no dirt stains on it.

"How'd he do that?" she asked Jake, amazed.

Jake smiled.

The kids oohed and aahed. "It's that easy, kids. "This is a trick, but Jesus doesn't have to use tricks like that. You ask Him, and Jesus will help you do the right things. Now, who wants a piece of candy?"

The clown stood up and walked over to pick up a big bag and pass out candy. Parents and kids stood. Maggie took that to mean the show was over.

"He's talented," Maggie said, impressed. "Did you see how those kids were listening to him? I didn't know they had anything like this here. Is that what you do on Saturdays?"

Jake chuckled. "Actually, you guessed it. Our clown here comes out once a month to talk to the kids. But you've already met him."

As if just noticing them, the clown looked up, smiled and waved.

"I have?" Maggie asked.

Jake nodded. "You have. That's my friend who towed your car. Tyler Jenson. He's from Texas but has lived here almost ten years now."

Maggie's eyes widened. "I had no idea. His makeup is really good."

"If you have him, why do you need my help?"

"I need help with the puppets and passing out candy and a myriad of other things, including someone to sit by the kids or listen when they have to whisper something to someone, or hold them if they fall asleep. The list is endless. That's what Shirley did.''

Maggie watched the kids take the candy, hug Tyler, chatter back and forth with their parents, and suddenly didn't know if she could do it.

She felt like such a fraud. Her relationship with her parents wasn't like this. Those mothers responded so loving and gentle. She was going to be a parent, too, unless she put her child up for adoption. With the way she'd been raised, would she be a good parent?

If she couldn't, what made her think she could she give these little kids what they needed?

"We'll take it one step at a time."

Jake's soft voice snapped her back to the present. She glanced at him, wondering how he knew what she'd been thinking. "I don't know if I can, Jake. I have nothing left in me except bitterness."

Maggie wondered why in the world she would confess something like that to this near stranger with the compassionate eyes.

That was it. It was his eyes. She'd never seen eyes like that before.

"You do have more, Maggie-May," Jake said gently. "It's just going to take you time to realize that."

"You don't understand. It seems that everything I touch turns bad." Maggie struggled, trying to believe, but she was scared.

Thankfully, Tyler Jenson interrupted.

"I see you brought your new helper by."

Jake stared at her a moment longer, his eyes probing, before he turned to Tyler and shook his hand. "I wanted you to meet her—again. Or rather, I suppose I should say I wanted her to meet the real you."

Tyler chuckled. "Nice to meet you again, Maggie."

Maggie remembered. "You helped me with my car."

"That I did." Tyler smiled, then turned to Jake. "I'll see you Saturday, then?"

Jake nodded.

"Bye," Maggie said.

Tyler waved as he walked off.

"That's why you brought me down here?"

Jake shook his head. "I wanted to see your reaction to a bunch of kids in an open area." Jake pointed to the six or seven benches with the huge animals to climb on and nothing else to keep the kids in one area.

"And?" she asked, certain he was disappointed in her.

He smiled. "You did wonderfully."

Maggie dumped the last bit of her cone in the trash. "How can you say that? When I saw all those kids I realized I probably can't handle it at all."

"Exactly."

Jake looked longingly at his cone, then tossed it, too.

"You didn't have to do that," she said, even as he turned and started walking back toward the car.

"We should get you home for the night. Your job starts later than most, but you should get extra rest."

"I—"

"If you had been overconfident or blasé about the entire thing, Maggie, then I would have worried. But the concern mirrored on your face told me you care about kids and the position you'll be in when you're helping me with them. That's the most important thing. Everything else can be learned. True caring and compassion can't."

"But I can't do what Tyler did. The kids aren't going to listen to me."

"Maggie, Maggie," Jake said, taking her hand and guiding her toward the car. "I didn't ask you to be Tyler. God didn't ask you to be Tyler. Just be yourself. They'll listen to you. I guarantee it."

He smiled confidently.

Maggie remembered what she'd seen and returned the smile weakly, hoping he was right.

Chapter Seven

He was dead wrong.

These kids were nothing like those sweet little angels in the park. In a short time Maggie had seen one lob a rock at someone, then run off, another bite the finger of the child next to her and yet another tie a little girl's hair in knots.

And these kids didn't sit still. Oh, for Tyler they had eagerly followed him. But now they jumped and shouted during his story.

It didn't seem to faze him, or Jake, who calmly walked over and picked up a child who was trying to poke the kid next to him in the ear with a stick. He set the child down on his lap and continued to listen as if this were a regular occurrence. He encircled the other one with an arm and acted as if the child hadn't just tried to make the other one deaf.

He looked handsome in his jeans and blue shirt.

Maggie had noticed that first thing. Perfectly at home, somehow.

"Hey, lady," a small child who had stationed herself by her side when she arrived said, interrupting Maggie's thoughts.

"Yes, Tonika?" she asked.

The little girl was rubbing Maggie's tummy— again. "How come your stomach keeps moving around like that? It looks all crooked now. See that?"

Maggie glanced down to where Tonika was poking and saw the bulge of an elbow or knee.

"That's 'cause she's pregnant, you idiot."

Ah, the heckler. She'd been watching the young boy move around the crowd for the past fifteen minutes, interrupting, scolding the other kids, being a general nuisance. "That's not nice to say, Eddie," she said. She had a feeling he was just wanting attention.

"Why not? You're pregnant. My big sister is, too. I know what it looks like. That's the baby kid kicking."

Eddie had short, curly black hair and deep-brown eyes that twinkled mischievously when he was being loud. Right now they looked way too old for those of a ten-year-old child.

"I meant 'idiot,' Eddie. That's not nice. Apologize."

Maggie hated that word and didn't like the way Tonika's face had fallen when Eddie had called her that. She had been patient with the young boy, but she wouldn't tolerate his calling Tonika names.

He shrugged. "Hey, it's no skin off my nose.

Sorry, Tonika. You just ain't been around this none, I suppose.''

Tonika sniffled, but when Maggie's stomach suddenly moved again, Tonika forgot her hurt feelings and went back to feeling Maggie's rounded bulge again.

Maggie had no idea how the seven-year-old girl had ended up in her lap, but she continued to sit there, rubbing the protruding mound with abject fascination, doing her best to get the baby to move.

Jake glanced over and smiled, giving her a thumbs-up just before he stood and nonchalantly went back to work the puppets.

Eddie snickered and pointed, having seen Jake's move. Maggie shot him a dark look. "Don't do it," she warned when he started to shout out what he'd seen.

Eddie eyed her and then finally shrugged, turning away. What a little turkey, she thought. Immediately guilt assailed her. Maggie had never been down to this part of town. Earlier, when they'd been going door-to-door to the houses Jake seemed to know so well, Maggie had been appalled at how poor some of these people were.

Eddie had come from one such house. The sister he spoke of couldn't even be fifteen and had sneered at them. The mother had been on the couch asleep. Eddie had been cooking lunch.

The puppet show started with Tyler talking and Jake playing the part of a talking cow. Jake had told her he'd do the puppets first, just to show her how they interacted and what they usually did. He assured her there was no set pattern. The puppets taught a memory verse, joked around with the kids and made a point of backing up the story. That was it.

Toward the end, when they brought out the second puppet to make another point of the story and tie the memory verse back in, she was to sneak back there and work it. Really easy, he'd told her.

Yeah, she thought, right. If you had a quick wit and vivid imagination.

Maggie shifted as the baby made itself known in a most uncomfortable way, and she suddenly realized she was going to have a problem being out on the streets like this as her pregnancy advanced.

"Hey, lady, what's the matter?"

Maggie blinked and looked down at Tonika, then blushed when she saw the girl staring at her so knowingly. "Nothing, dear."

"You gotta go, don'tcha?" the girl persisted.

Maggie saw other kids glance at her, then back at what was going on up front. Figuring there was no reason to lie, she nodded. "I sure do."

If she thought that would end it, she was wrong. "I gotta go, too."

Patiently Maggie smiled and shushed the girl. "Let's not disturb Pastor Jake or his helpers."

"You can go to my house with me."

Maggie sighed, nodded and stood, thinking it'd be good to get the young girl away, since the crowd had finally quieted and was listening to what was being said. "Okay, that sounds great."

She was surprised when the young girl grabbed her hand and led her along to her house as though she were a long-lost friend. Tonika pulled out a key and opened the door.

The house was poor. Maggie noted that immediately. It reminded her of her own house currently. However, despite the lack of money, the house was also neat and spotless, and obviously filled with love; Maggie saw tiny little personalized things from Tonika hanging about everywhere, as well as small comforts for the little girl. "Tonika, where is your mom?"

Tonika shrugged. "She had to go to work today. I'm not allowed to leave except for Pastor Jake's show. Since you're with the group, my mama won't mind me bringing you in."

"You don't stay here alone, do you?"

Again Tonika shrugged. "Miss Emmaline next door keeps a watch on me. If I get bored, she lets me come over there."

Maggie gaped, unsure what to say. She was horrified, but understood the need of the parent to bring in money. Absently Maggie lay a hand on top of her own child, thinking how she might be in that very position one day.

If she kept the child.

Pain pierced her heart, not only from memories of the conception of the child but at the thought of any child living like this, too.

"It's in here," the little girl said, pointing. Then she followed the words with action by running into the bathroom and slamming the door.

She was back in a short time. "You can use it, too, but don't forget to wash your hands."

Maggie chuckled at the admonishment. "Thank you, Tonika, I won't."

Maggie slipped into the bathroom. When she finished washing her hands and went back out, Tonika was finishing up a glass of milk. "I'm ready!"

With renewed energy, the little girl ran to the door.

Maggie followed. She watched, impressed, as Tonika closed the door and made sure it was locked. Then she changed from grown-up to kid and took off skipping down the street, carefree again.

Thoughts swirled in Maggie's head about her own unborn child, thoughts she'd never faced before. Since finding out she was pregnant she had functioned on autopilot, not certain what to do, just surviving as the child developed within her. She had never really acknowledged that there was a child, other than realizing her own body was changing to accommodate it.

Now for the first time, seeing this child who was raised by a mother who was obviously single, Maggie faced the truth that she was in the same situation. She was pregnant, alone and was going to have a baby.

She would very likely end up working like this mother and have to leave her child. Could she do that if she decided to keep the baby?

Too many questions and too many emotions were opened up thinking about that. She didn't want to deal with the pain those questions brought. Didn't want to deal with the decisions she had to make.

So, instead, she concentrated on what was going on at that moment.

Back in the park, Jake held up a picture of a

chicken with several chicks around it and patiently explained how the mother was trying to protect the chicks from a fire that would consume them if they didn't run to her.

One chick was being stubborn, though, he went on.

Maggie realized it was nearing the time she was supposed to move behind the little stage to work the puppets.

Tyler gave her a cue from the audience, nodding toward the back of the stage.

Nervously she nodded.

Maggie went back behind the small wooden stage and looked around. A box of puppets set beneath the curtained window. On the back of the wood was taped a script of what was scheduled and when her puppet was supposed to appear.

As Maggie listened to Jake talking about how the mama chicken gave her life saving those chicks, her heart rate accelerated.

What was she doing here?

How could she do this?

She'd never worked with children before. Not like this. Nor had she ever been in this part of town. You couldn't fool streetwise kids like this. They were going to know she was a fake. They were going to know she had no idea what she was doing.

Sweat slicked her palms as she reached for the little girl puppet and slipped it on her arm.

Experimentally, Maggie moved the mouth of the puppet, feeling awkward as she did. Kneeling down, she put it by the edge of the curtain, waiting and listening. "Help me, Father. I have no idea what to do," she said.

"You're gonna chicken out, aren't you?"

Maggie jumped, turning her head in surprise. "Eddie! What are you doing here?" She whispered the question, very aware of the kids on the other side of the curtain.

Eddie's hand was on the stage. One push and she'd be exposed. She paled. Maggie didn't want this ruined for the other kids or Jake.

"I thought so. You don't look like no inner-city worker that's been here before. Brother Jake's friend Shirley was better. You don't even know how to use no puppet."

Maggie stared at Eddie, then sighed. "You're right, Eddie. I don't."

What could she do? Lie to the kid? He saw too much as it was.

With a disgusted look, Eddie strode over, dropped down next to her, grabbed a puppet and then stuck his arm up out of the curtain.

Only then did she realize Jake had knocked twice on the stage, trying to get someone to answer the door.

Eddie screwed his face up and made his voice crackle as he said, "Yeah, who is it? Who is it?"

Maggie realized he had on a grandma puppet.

Dumbfounded, she stared.

Eddie, the troublemaker, actually helping?

She shook her head.

"Well, hello, Grandma," Jake said from the other

side of the curtain. "I was just telling these kids about how a chicken gave up her life to save her babies."

"Oh, babies? Babies? I know all about them. Let me tell you, ain't that the truth, them good for nothing babies needing saving."

Maggie gulped; not sure where Eddie was going, she stuck her own puppet up.

"Just like this one," Grandma said, while Eddie grinned at her nastily from behind the scenes.

Maggie glared back. "I don't need saving," she said with the puppet.

Of course Eddie couldn't pass that up, and went into a long speech about how this young'un had almost broken her neck on roller blades and a car. Maggie was dumbfounded at the story Eddie spun.

Then Jake led the puppet show back to the memory verse. "You know, Grandma, your story reminds me of a verse about God sending His son. Do you or maybe your granddaughter know that one?"

Maggie opened her mouth to reply, but again Eddie beat her to it.

"Of course I do. God so loved the world that He gave His only begotten son that whoever believed in Him would have eternal life."

Maggie grinned, thinking that was close but not an actual quote. And Jake had planned to use only the first half of the verse. But still, that Eddie knew it impressed and humbled her.

"That's right, Grandma. God so loved the world…"

Jake turned back to the kids and had them repeat the phrase, then mentioned finding it in *John* 3:16.

Before Maggie could decide if Eddie had saved the show or not, Jake turned back and spoke to the grand-daughter. "You should remember that, too, Nelly. And that He'll save you and protect you, just as He did today when He kept you from getting run over by that car when you were roller blading."

Maggie replied, though she wasn't sure what, and then they pulled their hands back from the curtain.

She removed the puppet and dropped it into the box, staring at Eddie.

Eddie wouldn't meet her eyes. Instead, he pulled off the puppet, his little chin going up in the air as he stuffed his hands in his pockets.

Something gave in Maggie's heart as she realized this was all a mask, a wall of protection Eddie had built up around himself.

"Thank you," Maggie said softly, her heart opening up to the young boy.

Eddie shrugged. "I didn't do nothing except show Tonika how stupid you was not to know how to do puppets."

Eddie nonchalantly gave her a hug, totally surprising her, then resumed the tough look on his face and sauntered off.

Maggie shook her head, not offended by Eddie's words but perhaps understanding that he was protecting himself.

Maggie sat there watching as Eddie took up his place near the back of the audience.

Then it was over, and Eddie took off at a run to go play.

Tonika got up and hurried home. Several of the

other children all ran up and hugged Jake and the clown and got a few more candy treats before they left.

Then Jake came to where she stood, while Tyler broke down the stage and loaded it into the truck.

"You did great!"

Surprised, Maggie looked at Jake. "Please don't lie, Jake. I did miserably."

Genuinely surprised, Jake replied, "Maggie, you did not. Whatever gave you that idea?"

Maggie motioned toward the stage that Tyler was loading into the truck. "I froze and had no idea what to do."

Jake actually laughed. "Is that what it felt like to you? You did fine on this side. And what's more important, Eddie helped you."

Confused, Maggie asked, "Why is that so important?"

Jake smiled softly. "Eddie is one tough nut to crack. He doesn't take to others too much. If he came back there and helped, regardless of what he said, that means he's taken to you."

"I find that hard to believe," Maggie said, shaking her head.

"Believe it." Jake slipped a hand to the small of Maggie's back and guided her toward the truck. "Eddie has grown up in a rough area. He doesn't have role models. Eddie is the one basically taking care of the family. It's a very sad situation. He doesn't have a lot of respect for adults because of that. However, for some reason, all day he's been eyeing you strangely."

Jake opened the door and gently lifted her up into the truck. He smiled at her before he got in next to her. "To be honest, as I watched today, I think the reason he was so curious about you is simply that you cared enough to talk to him like an adult and correct him when he was teasing the other kids."

"I don't remember liking discipline," Maggie said, "I didn't like the way he picked at Tonika, either."

Jake chuckled. "That Tonika. She is a pill. She and Eddie go at it like they were really siblings. Sometimes Eddie does get carried away though and hurts her feelings."

"Well, he did today."

Jake nodded. "You made him apologize?"

Maggie nodded firmly.

"Good. I'm glad to hear that. He needs to learn it's okay to make a mistake and apologize. Just like Tonika needs to hear him say he's sorry."

Jake started the truck and headed back toward the church. "I remember, though, one incident where Tonika had him by the ears and he was hollering his head off. When I broke them apart and asked what she was doing, she informed me he'd said something to her and she was pinning his ears back for it. Evidently, that's one of her mother's favorite sayings when Tonika misbehaves."

Jake laughed.

Maggie watched him as he chuckled, thinking how carefree he looked when he laughed like that.

"I'm surprised."

Still smiling, Jake turned inquisitive eyes on her. "What?"

Maggie hadn't meant to say that out loud. "I, well, you seem so happy and free. With all the responsibilities I've seen you handle so far, how do you do it?"

Jake shook his head, his smile fading a bit. "I wish, Maggie-May, that I could say I was carefree and had no problems or didn't worry. But this center we're building—it means everything to me."

Maggie watched the rest of his smile fade as he scanned the traffic while he drove.

"I didn't mean to force the smile from your face."

He glanced at her, giving her a quirky grin. "You didn't. It's hard to explain what the center means to me."

His eyes went back to the traffic as he circled around onto the interstate. "I suppose it's because I grew up on the streets just like Eddie and Tonika and all the others. I want this center built. I want a place where kids can go to get off the streets, a place that's an alternative to the gangs and drugs, a place where the kids can get the Word of God and have a safe place to play."

Maggie noted the way he gripped the steering wheel, the determined glint in his eye, and realized she'd found his goal in life.

"It means a lot to you?" she questioned softly.

"Yes," he replied.

Maggie leaned back against the seat, gazing at the traffic, thinking woe to anyone who came between this man and his goal to see the center built.

There was a lot more to Jake than met the eye. The

light-hearted man had been replaced with one full of steely determination.

"Why is it so important?" Maggie probably shouldn't ask, but she couldn't curb her curiosity.

Jake didn't glance at her, and she didn't need to see his face to interpret what he was feeling when he replied, in a flat voice.

"So other kids won't end up like my kid brother. You see, while I was a teenager strung out on drugs, my kid brother was shot to death playing kick ball in the street."

Chapter Eight

"Oh, Jake!" Maggie reeled from Jake's words. "I'm so sorry."

"It was a long time ago. I'm over it now," he said, shrugging. He exited the highway and started the last short journey toward home.

He wasn't over it, though. Maggie could see plainly the truth written all over his demeanor whether he admitted it or not. "It wasn't your fault," she said gently.

Jake laughed, but the laugh was one of buried grief. "We'll never know if he would still be alive had I not been so out of it. Kids playing on the streets in neighborhoods like that." Jake shook his head. "I want to give others a chance, since my brother didn't have one."

"It's a wonderful goal," she murmured, touching her stomach as she did. Her being pregnant certainly wasn't going to endear him to the people at his church. What if they decided not to give any more money to help him get this center built? She knew things like pregnancy and her working for him would cast a bad light on a pastor, whether the child was his or not.

"You're worried about your pregnancy?"

Jake's soft query sounded like the snap of a whip in the truck. How had he known that?

Surprised, Maggie stared.

He nodded toward her stomach. Only then did she realize she was rubbing it.

Flushing, she shrugged. "A bit, I suppose."

Jake studied her until the light changed, then he turned his attention forward again. "Are you worried about the baby in general or how it's going to affect my job?"

The man was very astute. Maggie decided it must be that he worked with people on a regular basis and had to interpret what they didn't say as much as what they did—that, or God was giving him some extra help.

"Both."

Silence fell.

Maggie shifted.

They turned onto the country road that led to the church at the edge of town before Jake broke the silence. "There is no reason for you to worry about my job, Maggie. As for the other, I'm more than willing to listen if you want to talk."

Dark memories swirled in Maggie's mind of the conception of the child and all the indecision and fear since. How she would love to confide in someone, but she had learned what that meant—and just how people responded.

No, she couldn't, wouldn't, confide. "I'm fine on that, too. I don't need anyone to talk to."

She stared out the window.

Jake glanced over at her, his brow furrowed. He wondered if she realized how her voice lifted slightly when she lied.

He'd watched her all day. She was good with the kids, a little awkward at having never worked around them, but there was a tenderness she projected when the children approached her. It was no wonder the kids swarmed to her.

He couldn't believe she didn't realize it. But she didn't.

His little secretary had no idea how maternal she was—to every kid except the one she carried.

When he had pointed out the way she rubbed her stomach she stopped.

Curiosity ate at him—and not entirely on a professional level.

Maggie was very attractive. Her gentle spirit had distracted him more than once today. The husky laugh when one of the kids had said something amusing made his mind go blank more than once.

Jake shook his head, certain he had gone off the deep end. What was the matter with him? His mind had been wandering all day to Maggie and her voice, her smile, her life.

He felt just a bit guilty for hoping Maggie would confide in him a moment ago. Yes, he would listen professionally and offer prayer and advice, but he admitted it was the man in him who wanted to know.

Whose child did she carry? Was she in love with the man still? She wore no ring, though it looked like one might have been worn there before. Was Maggie divorced, then? And if she was, why?

He didn't like that curiosity ate at him this way, nor that, despite how standoffish Maggie acted, he still found himself attracted to her.

He'd been so distracted by Maggie that he'd actually told her about his kid brother and the problem he'd had with drugs. How many people did he discuss his past with? Yet, with Maggie, it'd seemed natural to be honest with her.

Wearily he shook his head again. It was none of his business, and he shouldn't push her.

He glanced over again and saw her pleating the bottom of her top with two fingers and decided Maggie had no idea she was doing it. Maggie wasn't the type to show emotion. She hurt. It shone in her eyes. When he'd asked about the child, her eyes went blank and she smiled. The look she gave everyone, including him when he tried to get close, drove him crazy.

"Do you have a doctor?"

Maggie blinked, then turned to him, smiling, that same blank expression in her eyes. "I've been going to the clinic when I could. Unfortunately, I've had some trouble driving standard, so I can't make the appointments."

Jake frowned. "That's not good. You shouldn't have to miss seeing the doctor."

"It's only driving long lengths. My legs get tired

and cramp up. I'm worried about wrecks in heavy traffic. Short legs and a big stomach don't mix.''

Jake turned into the driveway and stopped at his house. He hopped out and came around to her door and opened it, then reached up to help her down. Despite her shape, she was light, which concerned him. ''Tell you what, Maggie-May. You make that appointment, and I'll see you get to it on time.''

He smiled at the surprise in her eyes, glad to see an honest reaction.

''Oh, no, I couldn't trouble anyone...I mean, babies are babies and they grow and don't really require all the fuss doctors say they do.''

Jake took Maggie's elbow and walked her over to her house, his concern growing again. At the porch he stopped and looked down at her. Corkscrew curls danced around her face where they'd fallen from the clip at the base of her neck. Wide green eyes stared up at him so solemnly. ''Why are you scared to face the existence of the child, Maggie?''

She paled, her lips parting slightly. ''I—I—I'm not.''

Jake studied her, felt the tremor in her. He shouldn't have asked her. The reality of the child brought pain to her for some reason. It wasn't his business. Yet seeing that pain, the helplessness in her eyes as she stood there refusing to respond to his query, twisted his heart.

''You don't have to tell me. But I'm not taking no for an answer regarding the doctor's appointment. Call, then let me know when the appointment is.''

He thought from the way the end of her nose turned

pink that she was holding back tears but couldn't be sure. Leaning forward he brushed his lips across her forehead, a purely platonic action.

It disconcerted him, though, when the fruity smell of shampoo drifted from her hair, catching his attention, and the warm vanilla scent of her perfume wrapped itself around him.

Confused, he pulled back. "I'll be in the office doing some work. If you can get the clinic on the line today, give me a call. Otherwise, I'll expect to hear something on this subject Monday."

Maggie's cheeks were pink, which made Jake feel even more the fool. Why in the world had he kissed her on the forehead?

Admit it, you fool, he thought, disgusted. You're attracted to her.

He stepped back and turned, before going down the steps. Jake told himself he couldn't be attracted to her. There were too many problems. He didn't know whose baby Maggie carried and if she was over that man. He didn't know if she was even interested in a relationship. And besides, he had so much work to do on the center he didn't have time for dating.

Father, I have got to be out of my mind. Please help me just redirect my thinking back to where it should be.

Jake found it didn't help to say that. His mind was still on the softly rounded figure of the woman he'd left on the front steps of her house.

Maggie went into her house dumbfounded and a little nervous by what had just happened.

"Don't read anything into it. The man was just showing you compassion."

But it'd been so long since anyone had touched her in any way. She'd forgotten how nice it could feel to have someone take her elbow or help her out of a car.

Of course, with her bulk, she needed help now to get out of a truck. But still, it felt good. When Jake had touched her shoulders and placed that soft kiss on her forehead she had almost burst into tears.

He had no idea what she had gone through, or was going through, yet he'd offered her comfort. Although she had trouble believing he kissed all his flock on the forehead.

Maggie grinned thinking of him trying to kiss Tyler on the head, then sniffed as her eyes filled with tears.

"Meeewwooooorrrr."

The pitiful sound of Captain Kat broke through the bittersweet pain she was experiencing.

"Kathryn! I didn't forget about you," Maggie said, though she temporarily had.

She went over and carefully squatted down to slip her hands under the cat and lift her.

The cat hissed, then growled at her. "Now, you just stop that, Captain Kat. I won't put up with it. You're not going to get your way on this. I happen to know you need help, and you're going to get it whether you want it or not."

Maggie thought of Jake's attitude and reddened. "This is different," she said, and set the cat over in the litter box. "You have to do this," she told the cat before pushing herself up and going into the kitchen to get the cat fresh water and food. "I—"

Maggie poured the food and then the water. "I don't really need him. Besides, you know what'll happen. Eventually, someone is going to see me, and my parents will try to cause problems. If they don't, well then, his church surely will because of the child and my single status."

Maggie carried the food back into the room and lifted the cat out of the box, ignoring the growl.

She placed Captain Kat back on the pillow. "There you go. Here're some food and water. You just rest."

Maggie grabbed up the litter box and dumped the contents in the commode, then returned the box next to the cat.

Maggie got the antiseptic solution the doctor had given her and set to work carefully cleaning the wounds on the cat.

"Still," she said, musing softly as she cleaned the cat, "wouldn't it be wonderful if there really was such a thing as happily ever after on this earth?"

Maggie thought about the verse that said with God all things were possible. She believed that; she really did.

Then she looked down at her stomach, remembered what her parents and her former fiancé had said and sighed.

But in this case, Maggie didn't think there was much hope.

Chapter Nine

Maggie clasped her hands nervously, glancing sideways at Jake, who was slipping in and out of traffic.

"I'd never expect you to drive a midsize car."

Jake glanced at her and laughed.

She liked the tiny crinkles that appeared around his eyes, the way his dimples showed. "Thought because all I rode around in was a truck..."

She shook her head. "I just hadn't seen this."

Jake glanced back around, changing lanes. "This is a car that I saved a long time for. It's expensive, well okay, expensive for my income, but I know I'll have it ten years down the road."

Maggie considered how a year ago she wouldn't have been caught in a car like this. And would never have driven the same car for over a year. Of course, this car was much better than the small piece of barely running metal she owned now.

How attitudes change, she acknowledged, looking out to see how much farther they had to go.

"So tell me, Maggie. Who is this doctor of yours? How long has he been practicing?"

Maggie glanced back at Jake, surprised. Studying him, she couldn't see anything in his face to indicate why he had asked. She decided to tell him. "*She* is a very good doctor. She really does care for the people here, but she's overworked, just like all the other doctors who work the clinic." Maggie sighed. "I feel lucky to have been placed with her."

"You didn't get to choose your doctor."

Maggie recognized the statement was not meant as a question, but she answered anyway. "No. At a free clinic you don't have a choice."

Jake pulled into the parking lot and got out of the car, then walked around the dark-mauve hood to open her door.

Maggie appreciated it, appreciated the help when he reached in for her hand, appreciated the fact that he didn't laugh at her when she struggled out.

Flushing, she said, "I feel like an ox."

Jake smiled softly. "You look like an angel."

Maggie blinked, then laughed. "Oh, I think I'll keep you around just to hear things like that."

Though she had said it, she was suddenly very aware of Jake as more than just her employer or the pastor of the church she'd gone to Sunday. He was very much a person who had feelings and emotions.

Curiously, she had to wonder if he really meant his sweet words or was only flattering her. She hoped it was the latter, knowing how dangerous it would be for him to fall for someone like her.

Maggie quickly scooped her purse and slung it over her shoulder before turning to the clinic.

"I have to get my records and then go down to the last waiting room on the right."

Jake nodded.

"You've been here before?"

"With various people from the church, yes."

Well, there went her hope that he was treating her differently. Of course she was rather relieved, wasn't she? He threw her already roiling emotions right back into turmoil with his next words.

"I go everywhere, Maggie, when I'm called."

She wondered if he meant just with others or her included. Deciding she could beat herself to death over the subject, she determined to take it how it was probably meant. "That's your job. To help those of us who need it."

Jake frowned as Maggie started down the hall.

That was not what he'd meant at all. Actually, he was surprised with the conversation today. Jake always put his work first.

Time didn't permit him to disrupt his work now to flirt with a woman who was surely still hurting over the desertion of an ex-boyfriend or husband.

He'd do best to remember that. Of course, Jake wondered, when did he ever do what was considered *best?*

If he'd done what was best he wouldn't be seeing the dream of his heart fulfilled—a center for kids. Nor would he even be where he was today when everyone he'd known had told him he wasn't really called to preach, to find something else, something that someone who hadn't been all messed up could do.

Jake shrugged. Maggie was hurting. No matter what he felt, he wouldn't act on it until her heart had time to heal.

He walked into the lobby and took a seat next to where Maggie sat.

"It shouldn't be long," Maggie whispered.

She looked around. She hadn't missed the glances of some of the other women when Jake had walked in. Several raised appraising eyebrows. Maybe he didn't realize it, but she was certain those women thought Jake was the father. She wasn't sure which embarrassed her more—that she was single and pregnant, like many of the women here, or that they thought the pastor had fathered...

"You flush any brighter and we'll just switch these lights off, Maggie-May, and let your face light the room."

The softly spoken words from Jake had her warming all the way down her neck.

He chuckled sensually. "Let me guess. You're embarrassed because they probably think I'm the father. Or is it because I'm a pastor and they think I'm the father?"

Maggie couldn't help the involuntary reaction to his words.

He reached over and took her hand, patting it gently. "Pastors do have children, too, I'm told."

"Stop it," she said, her embarrassment obvious in her words.

"I'm sorry, Maggie. I'm simply a man. That's all they know, so don't worry about what they think."

"The Bible says avoid all appearance of evil," Maggie whispered.

Jake started coughing, covering his mouth.

"You're laughing," she lamented.

"I didn't realize this would bother you so much. I can't help it. You're quoting Scriptures to me."

He chuckled again, and she reached over and slapped his arm, mortified. "Will you cut it out?"

His grin was infectious, though. Before long she was grinning.

When they recovered, he smiled at her. "Maggie, sitting in a waiting room with a pregnant woman is not evil."

Maggie had to admit, when he said it in that tone, it sounded silly. "But what if they know you are a pastor and they see you with me and…"

"Maggie." Jake's eyes turned serious. "I live in a glass house it's true. But all I can do is live my life as I feel God would want me to. I can't live it the way others want me to. If I did, I would constantly have to change how I lived because someone would find something wrong with every single thing I did. Believe me, I have already been through most anything you could imagine at one time or another."

Maggie lifted a brow skeptically. "Even hiring a single pregnant woman as your secretary? Having her working with you at the children's ministry and then taking her to appointments?''

"Well, there you've got me. This is the first time for that. Don't worry. If I hadn't felt a peace in my heart about it, you never would have gotten the job.''

"You're saying you think God wanted you to give me the job?'' Maggie couldn't believe he was saying this.

He smiled. "Yes, I do.''

"Well, just don't get too comfortable. I probably won't be around too long.''

Maggie's eyes widened when she realized what she'd said.

Jake frowned. "You're not thinking of running out on me, are you?''

Maggie was relieved he thought that. He couldn't know about her parents. "No, Jake. I'm not. I just imagine in a month or two you'll get tired of me and be ready to hire someone who doesn't have to miss work all the time for appointments and take breaks in the afternoon to prop up her feet.''

"Dadadada…''

Maggie looked down at the small child who had toddled up to Jake.

Jake turned and grinned at the blond-haired, blue-eyed cherub slobbering all over his pants and patting them with the wet hand she'd been chewing on. "Well now, hello there, little one.''

Jake glanced up to see who the baby might belong to and spotted one mother with a child similar in looks, changing the child's diaper.

A Mother's Love

"Dadadada…"

The child patted his leg again and then proceeded to crawl up onto his lap.

Jake chuckled. "Dadadadadadadada to you, too."

The child chortled, clapping her hands.

Jake bounced his knee, keeping a firm grip on her as he made soft silly noises, just long enough until the mother turned to check her other child and noted her gone.

Maggie was enchanted. She watched Jake hand the child back over and the child fuss, not wanting to leave. Jake tickled the child's belly.

The baby chortled again.

"Ms. Garderé?"

Maggie glanced over and saw the nurse. "Yes?"

She started to push herself up, but Jake was suddenly there, helping her.

"I'm not an invalid," she said, her cheeks turning pink.

Jake paused, studying her. "I know that. And I think you know that, too."

"Jake, I…"

"Right this way," the nurse interrupted.

Maggie turned and went in for the doctor's appointment, wishing she could have apologized for what she'd said.

Through her entire appointment, where they measured her, checked the baby, listened to the heartbeat and asked a million questions, her attitude toward Jake still weighed heavily on her mind.

When she went back out, she intended to apologize,

but stopped at what she saw. Sitting over in the corner with a woman was Jake, holding the woman's hand as she cried softly.

He was simply a man. He'd said that.

But how many men did she know who would feel comfortable enough to sit and comfort a total stranger, especially a woman while she cried her heart out to him?

Jake suddenly looked right at her, startling her. It was as if he'd sensed the moment she walked in. He nodded at her and then turned back to the woman.

Maggie moved toward them, sitting far enough away so she wouldn't overhear what was said.

Jake continued to talk until another person came up. The woman, who looked to be older than the one Jake sat with, plopped down and started talking. She wore a tailored outfit, very nice, with her hair pulled back in clips.

In a bit Jake squeezed the woman's hand and got up, saying a few more words before leaving.

Maggie was curious but wasn't sure if she should ask what had gone on.

They walked in silence to the car. Jake opened the door and helped her in, then went around and climbed in his side. Instead of starting the car, he sat, leaning his head against the steering wheel.

"Are you okay?"

Jake sighed and finally lifted his head. "The woman is carrying twins. They just told her the likelihood of her carrying both to term is almost 100 percent unlikely. They wanted to take one baby now so the other could have a chance.''

"Oh, no," Maggie said, her heart flip-flopping.

Jake nodded. "She doesn't want to lose the chances of a child but refuses to consider abortion, either."

Maggie nodded. "God's hands."

"Yeah. I prayed with her, talked with her, listened to her until J.J. got there. Then I turned her over to her."

"J.J.?"

Jake chuckled. "J.J. is the nickname she earned for telling everyone she meets it's 'Just Julie.' She is a pastor at one of the local churches. She's a dear, absolutely hilarious."

Maggie listened to the description of Just Julie and found herself mildly depressed, until his next words.

"She rules her three kids with an iron hand. And melts like butter on a grill when her husband smiles her way."

"The woman goes to her church?"

Jake nodded. "She had already called J.J. but needed someone to sit with her."

Maggie nodded. "Of course she did."

"Sorry to have kept you waiting."

Maggie studied Jake. "Why in the world would you apologize for comforting that woman?"

Jake glanced at her, then sighed. "Some people wouldn't appreciate it. Since I brought you here, it was rude of me to make you sit for an extra fifteen minutes when your appointment was over. It could have been an hour if J.J. had been unreachable for some reason."

"Jake. That's your job. That's just part of it."

Jake suddenly grinned. "It's nice to know you understand. It happens a lot."

Maggie smiled, remembering the tender look of understanding on Jake's face, and could see how it would. He cared. He really cared about people.

"How do you do it?"

Jake glanced over at Maggie. "Do what?"

"How do you care so deeply? Doesn't it ever get to you? The pain? The fears? The hurt?"

Jake sat still for a while, then finally started the car. "Yeah, it gets to me. But I have God, who knows what that feels like and takes that burden from me, wearing it Himself. I could let the pain and fear and stress consume me. Just like you could, Maggie. You could let your fears and pain over your problems consume you and you could hide away, stop coping. But God has promised His yoke is easy, His burden is light. All we have to do is go to Him."

Maggie nodded. She shifted around in the seat and put her seat belt on, thinking about what Jake said. God's yoke is easy, His burden is light, she thought. Even if it doesn't seem like it, He told us His grace was sufficient. She wondered when she'd forgotten that.

"Can I take you out to lunch?"

Jake's deep warm voice interrupted her thoughts and she looked over at him. She realized they were still sitting at the clinic. "Don't you have to get back to work?"

Jake chuckled. "I have to eat, too. I'm a growing boy. My stomach is telling me it's time to eat."

On cue, her stomach rumbled.

"Sounds like junior or juniorette is telling you something, also."

She laughed. "Don't be silly. That wasn't the baby. That was my stomach."

"Ah, then you're telling me you are hungry?"

Maggie smirked. "Oh, that was very funny. Get me to admit it's *my* stomach, then I can't argue."

He grinned. "It worked."

"Okay. That sounds good."

Maggie could enjoy the world of make-believe for a while. She could pretend everything was normal and she was out with a gorgeous hunk of a man on a lunch date.

Unfortunately, reality intruded with the huge lump that stuck out in front of her. Looking down at her stomach as Jake drove out of the parking lot, she touched her stomach softly.

Yes, she could pretend, but the truth wouldn't go away. She was a single, pregnant, alone.

"Do you still love him?"

"Who?" she asked, listening to the hum of the engine as the drove down the street.

"The father."

Memories of the last time she'd seen him, the time all her feelings had been shattered, played through her mind. "No," she whispered. "I don't love him."

"Good."

Surprised at Jake's reply, she met his gaze. "Why? Why good?"

Jake smiled before turning into a salad-and-soup shop.

"Because I find you different from any woman I've met. Because I can't imagine you wasting away hurting over some man who isn't here. Because you deserve better. Because there's so much out there for you. Choose one."

Because I care about you. That was what she would have chosen. But it wasn't one of the choices. Instead, she replied, "I'm carrying another man's child. I'm broke. The luck that follows me…"

She trailed off, unable to go on.

"You're carrying your child. You have a job, and God is all you need. Don't sell yourself short, Maggie. God made you special. He wants to heal your heart. Just let Him do it. Take it one step at a time."

He wants to heal your heart. Yes, she would suppose the pain in her heart did need healing. But what Jake didn't understand was with parents like hers, no matter how much he tried to help her, it was just going to fail in the end.

"I suppose so, Jake."

"I know so, Maggie. Now, I'm done lecturing. Let's go feed you and fatten you up."

Maggie jerked her gaze up to Jake's to see a soft look in his eyes that was at odds with his words.

"Fatten me up? What? Am I to be a sacrifice or something?"

Jake chuckled, sending shivers down her spine.

"Oh, Maggie. I love it when that sense of humor of yours breaks free. One day, one day—" he reached out and touched her cheek, his warm fingers bringing a feeling of safety to her "—yes, one day, I hope you can be much freer with that and not have to be prodded to let go."

Maggie stared into the deep dark eyes of the man in front of her and sighed, wishing the same thing, but as frozen up as she felt inside, she doubted that could ever happen.

To laugh and joke meant to trust. How could she trust or open up when she knew things could only end in disaster?

Chapter Ten

"Yoo-hoo?"

Maggie jumped, looking from where she was just finishing with the bandages on the cat.

"It's me, Jennifer. The day-care manager."

Maggie smiled and went to the door, not too surprised by the unexpected visit. "Hello, Jennifer. Come in."

Jennifer was dressed in a pair of jeans and a huge untucked man's shirt, her hair pulled up under a baseball cap. In her hands she carried a large plastic container with condensation on the outside.

"I was on my way to work. But you know, when I got there, I found I'd brought too many veggie snacks for the kids today. I knew you were pregnant and wondered if you would take these."

If that wasn't a lie, Maggie didn't know what was. But the way Jennifer smiled so sweetly kept Maggie from being embarrassed about the handout. "Thank you," she said softly. "I imagine this is like the orange juice two days ago?"

"No, we didn't have enough room then."

Maggie chuckled and shook her head. Jennifer had been by three times now since she'd been here. The woman was more like a child than a woman, in her opinion. She dressed so informally, got right down and played with the kids and was so...carefree.

Maggie wondered if she herself had ever been like that, tried to remember back a year ago and found it hard to fight past the pain. "Let me just put this up." Maggie walked into the kitchen.

"How's Kat?"

Maggie looked to where the cat lay growling, the whites of her eyes showing, and noted Jennifer didn't even blink at how the cat eyed her. She smiled. "Better."

"I thought so. Her growl is louder."

Maggie chuckled. "So, you noticed."

"I've heard all about this cat from Jake. He's certain one of these days you aren't going to show up for work and he's going to come over here and find you devoured by her."

Maggie switched the veggies—broccoli, squash, carrots, cauliflower—all to another dish and then rinsed out Jennifer's dish before drying it and returning it to her.

Maggie reached down and patted the cat. "So, Jake thinks Captain Kat is going to eat me, does he?"

Jennifer shoved the plastic container under her arm. "Yep. Of course, he was certain the gunrunners were going to get me on my way to San Gabriel. Jake worries, and is very protective of his own.''

Maggie felt her heart trip at those words. "His own?'' She laughed uneasily as she went to get her keys. "Well, I'm certainly not *his own*.''

"Just a saying. You're one of the church so you're one of *his own*.''

"Oh, yes. I—of course.'' Maggie blushed.

"He's always doing that, too,'' Jennifer said, going out the door.

"What's that?''

"Mistaking what I say. Why, just yesterday I said, 'Jake, you know I think you've developed a dependency on Maggie.'''

"You what?'' Maggie stopped on the porch and stared at Jennifer, dumbfounded. "That's ridiculous. He doesn't even know me. He—''

Jennifer chuckled. "Similar to what Jake said, until I mentioned the office and then he started singing your praises.''

Maggie flushed, then shook her head. "I doubt that. I can't figure out Shirley's filing system. It's driving me crazy.''

Maggie went carefully down the stairs and turned on the path to the church.

"Yeah, well, that's what Jake had to say. He also said you were doing admirably with it. You see, Shirley had her own system. Purchases she put under 'Bought.'''

"All of them?''

"Yep. All of them. And what was it...oh! Yes.

Sunday-school material was all placed under 'Teaching.'"

"Oh, dear."

Jennifer laughed, a soft sweet sound, which urged Maggie to join in. Maggie found herself automatically relaxing around Jennifer.

Over the past few days Maggie had found herself relaxing a lot. The people here were all nice. Only a couple had avoided her glance when she came in or when they came to speak to the pastor. Most engaged her easily in conversation, didn't treat her like a pariah and didn't ask questions.

But Jennifer—Jennifer topped the list of oddities. She treated Maggie like a long-lost sister. There were no questions, no strange looks. Not even a blink of the eye. Jennifer just laughed and then launched into a story.

Jennifer was an optimist, Maggie decided. She always smiled, never frowned, never said a bad word against anyone.

"How do you do it?" Maggie opened the back door of the church and went inside, sighing in relief as the cool air-conditioned air hit her humidity-soaked skin.

"Do what?" Jennifer asked, throwing her arms open and letting out a big "Ahhh" as the air hit her.

"Stay so...up? Haven't you ever been through anything to bring you down?" Maggie flushed. "I didn't mean to sound so bitter. I—I just..." Maggie trailed off, wishing the floor would open up and devour her.

"Don't be embarrassed." Jennifer reached out and

slipped an arm around Maggie's shoulders and hugged her.

Maggie was surprised at the action but didn't push her away as she might have anyone else.

Jennifer released her and started toward the office. Jake wasn't there. Jake spent the first couple of hours each morning praying and then went on hospital visits and anything of that nature.

"You know, Maggie. The Bible says to let God fight our battles. God is our refuge, our rock, the person we run to when we're scared or afraid. It took me a long time to learn that. But I did."

Jennifer smiled and went into Maggie's office. "And I really had to learn that lesson when my mother died and left me with her day-care center—a center no one would leave their kids at because I wasn't anything more than a kid myself. I had to learn it when one of those children was killed by snake bites because the mother couldn't afford to leave the child anywhere else, and I'd had to shut the center down."

Jennifer dropped into a chair and smiled softly up at Maggie. "And still, sometimes, I have to relearn the lesson when I allow things in my heart to fester instead of releasing them and going on."

Maggie turned to the filing cabinets, feeling the blood drain out of her face. "It's so hard sometimes."

"Yes, it is. But to go on, to live again, fall in love, trust, sometimes we have to let go of those hurts."

Maggie wondered how in the world the woman knew what was going on, then remembered Jennifer hadn't actually named what was going on in her heart, just pinpointed some of the problems. "Even if I do, Jennifer, it'll all end up going wrong in the end."

Maggie opened the drawer and stared at the files. She didn't hear Jennifer cross the carpet, only felt her small hand touch her shoulder. "Just trust God, Maggie. And Jake. It'll all work out."

Maggie nodded.

She didn't move until she heard the woman talking to someone out in the lobby, then she folded into her chair, her heart beating staccato.

"Good morning!"

Maggie jumped, grabbing at her chest. "Jake, you scared me to death!"

Jake slowed his tread, smiling at Maggie. "I might have to try that more often if it'll put color in your cheeks like that."

She flushed and his grin widened.

"Oh, you!" She yanked a tissue out of the box and tossed it at him.

He made a dodging grab for it just as she did. He ended up with her hand. To avoid pulling her arm out, he tried to compensate and ended up sprawled across her desk, his head in her chest.

Maggie gasped.

Jake jerked back, raking everything off the desk as he went.

When Maggie saw he was actually red, she laughed.

"I was getting ready to apologize. However, if it makes you laugh I'll attempt something else."

Maggie, who could tell her own cheeks were pink,

just shook her head. "What put you in such a good mood, and why are you in early today?"

Jake sighed and put on a mock frown as he scooped up the miscellaneous things he'd knocked off her desk. "Sounding like Shirley already. What is it? Does it have something to do with that chair? You sit in it and become bossy? Wait a minute—let me try it."

He started around the desk and Maggie held out a hand in protest. "Not one more step! If this chair is bossy, I'm going to keep it."

Jake stopped. "It was worth a try."

Leaning back against the edge of her desk, he smiled.

Maggie liked his smile. He wore a pair of khaki pants with a navy pullover.

All in all, the man looked great.

Realizing she was studying him, she forced her gaze up—and met his knowing grin.

Deciding to ignore it, she tried to bluff her way through. "I just wondered why you were, uh, so dressed up? Something special?"

Jake slowly nodded, his gaze traveling slowly over her. Maggie knew what he'd see. She was wearing a balloon dress, as she liked to call it. Powder blue with a bouquet of flowers right over the big protrusion in front of her. It had cute little cap sleeves and a scoop neck, then just ballooned out the rest of the way down.

She'd clipped her hair up with a pretty floral clip, but still it didn't help. She felt round and short.

She appeared like a pregnant woman who was about to drop her baby.

"You look beautiful today."

The softly spoken sentence astonished her, and she glanced at him with surprise.

It evidently shocked Jake, too, for he seemed disconcerted. Slowly, though, the odd expression left his face, to be replaced by a smile. Finally, he answered her question, not commenting again on how she looked. "Yes, I'm going somewhere today. I got a call. It's definite. We've been approved to build the project on the land we bought. These plans were accepted. I have to run out later and sign some paperwork. I'll want you to type special informational sheets for me, and letters. And I'd like you to go with me if you have a chance. It'll be after lunch."

Maggie nodded. "Of course."

Jake studied Maggie again. "You know, you really do look wonderful today. Your face looks fresh, relaxed. Strain lines that were there when you first started working here are gone."

"Gee, thanks." Maggie didn't mean to sound sarcastic, but that wasn't what a woman with swollen ankles wanted to hear.

Jake chuckled, reached out and chucked her under the chin. "Would you like to hear the rest of what I was thinking? I think the green of your eyes reminds me of the same color on hyacinth leaves and that the shade of lipstick you're wearing is like azaleas fresh in bloom and that when you smile like you were you could light up a whole room."

Maggie gulped, staring at Jake, feeling the warmth

of his hand imprinted on her chin. Though he continued to smile, she could see the seriousness in his eyes. "You're just being nice," she whispered.

Slowly he shook his head. "I don't lie, Maggie-May. It bothers me that you don't see your own beauty."

"But—but—but I'm pregnant!" She pointed at her stomach, flustered, stuttering over his words.

Jake smiled. "Are you now, sweetheart?" He looked down and his eyes widened as though he had just realized that. "Oh, my, when did that happen?" Putting a hand to his forehead, he shook his head. "And pregnant women are just so lovely...."

"Yeah, swollen ankles and all," she said, trying to joke and stop him before he ruined his nice words with a description of just how she really looked.

Jake paused, tilting his head slightly. "I wasn't teasing about that, Maggie. Watch most pregnant women you know. Most have a glow about them, a secret look as if they hold the future within them—which they do. I think God gave women a special blessing when He allowed them to be the bearer of life."

Maggie didn't know what to say. She touched her stomach, stunned by the beauty of Jake's words.

Jake eyed her stomach. "It's a special gift you carry, Maggie. Life. Don't ever let anyone belittle you about it. Mistakes are in the past. As long as they're under the blood, they no longer matter. Today, now, is what matters. Accept the gift God gave you and pray for it every day and think why you were so lucky to be blessed with such a gift."

The mood shattered at Jake's last words. "Lucky? A gift?" Maggie shook her head, pain and bitterness reminding her of just who she was and why her attraction could never go anywhere with Jake. "Thank you, Jake. I appreciate your words of encouragement."

She could tell Jake knew he'd said something to bother her. He didn't ask. Instead, after a moment he knelt near the credenza and pulled out the bottom drawer.

"Let's see what we can do with these files, shall we?"

Maggie gazed down at Jake. The shirt stretched over his wide shoulders, outlining muscles. The collar lay gently against his neck.

It just wasn't fair that a man should be so handsome. Especially her boss, her preacher, especially when she was pregnant. She sighed and turned to help him work.

She found it relatively easy to start rearranging the files with Jake's help. She also found she had a wonderful time later that day when she ran errands with him.

That night, as she lay in bed, she thanked God that she had such a good boss, and prayed that things would continue to look up.

Chapter Eleven

"He's possessed. How could I have ever thought him such a wonderful guy?"

Maggie sat on the porch, pulling off the last bandage from Captain Kat. "Tell me, Kathryn, how could I have believed it?"

The cat growled in return.

"I'm glad you agree. A town party. He expects me to attend a town party. Just because it'd be good for me to get out in—"

"That cat looks like she's had a bad hair day."

Maggie silently groaned before glancing over to where Jake was coming around the corner. He looked wonderful as usual, in a pair of jeans and a tucked-in polo shirt.

"She was hit by a car. Of course she looks like she's had a bad-hair day. She was shaved, and this is the first time most of the bandages have been off."

Jake stopped short of the cat, staying upwind, she

noticed. And he said he wasn't allergic. She shook her head.

"I just came to see if you're ready. I'm really glad you agreed to help at the town party."

Maggie sighed and stood, lifting the cat in her arms.

"She's growling." The low warning in Jake's voice brought a smile to Maggie's face.

"She always growls."

Jake shifted from foot to foot, eyeing the cat as if the creature were from another planet. "It might be a good idea to think of getting her declawed if you're going to keep her."

Maggie shook her head. "She needs her claws to defend herself. I wouldn't leave her helpless."

Jake studied Maggie before nodding. "Very well. Just be careful."

"I'm always careful."

When Jake opened his mouth to say something else, Maggie decided to change the subject. "Just what is it you need my help with at the town party today that no one else can do?"

Maggie went inside, hearing Jake's steps as he followed. The sound of the door closing behind her was loud in the silence. The silence, except for the continuing growl of Kathryn as Maggie took her over and put her back in her box.

"It's a surprise."

"Oh?" Maggie went in the kitchen to dump the bandages and wash up before returning to the living room. "The job is that bad, is it?"

Sheepishly, Jake shrugged. "I suppose I could have

gotten someone else, but I thought you'd have fun. If you don't mind, let's just keep it a secret until we arrive.''

Maggie studied him, curious. He appeared almost boyish in his excitement. Why hadn't she noticed that before?

A slow smile curved Maggie's lips, and a hand came to rest on her stomach as she watched him. Finally she nodded. "Very well. I won't ask.''

He grinned. "Good. Let's get going.''

Jake came up and slipped a hand to her back, urging her toward the door.

"My purse, Jake.''

Jake shook his head. "It'd only be in the way. You won't need it.''

Maggie sighed. "If you say so.''

"Trust me, Maggie-May.''

Maggie met his gaze. Dark eyes stared deeply into her own. A current of something passed through her and she knew, in that instant, that she could trust this man. She nodded. "I do.''

A slow smile curved his own lips. His focus dropped to her lips. Maggie felt her heart rate pick up and her breathing constrict.

Jake hesitated for a moment, then nodded. "I'm glad.''

He turned back to the door and Maggie sagged, released from the strange spell. If she didn't know better, she'd say that was old-fashioned attraction for Jake. But as she'd convinced herself before, it would do no good to think about such things, especially since they couldn't be reciprocated.

"Sorry, but we're in the church truck again."

Maggie, her attention drawn by Jake's voice, glanced up and saw the back of the truck filled with chairs, tables and other miscellaneous stuff.

He pulled open the door for her. "You just like watching me struggle in and out," she muttered as she stepped up to haul herself into the truck.

Jake chuckled, his hands going to where her waist would normally be. "Actually, it's an excuse to get my hands on you," he joked, then hefted her up.

"Oooaaafff." Maggie hit the seat with a thud.

She scowled at Jake. He only chuckled and slammed her door, then trotted around and climbed in.

"I feel like a cow."

Jake grinned. "Best-looking cow I've ever seen."

Maggie gaped. "I can't believe you said that."

Jake raised an eyebrow. "Oh? I said you were good-looking. You are the one, my dear, who said she was a cow."

Maggie shook her head. "You're in a mood today."

Jake backed around in a large U and then took off toward town. "The annual town races are a blast. It's a day the entire town opens up for people to visit, eat, have fun and mingle."

Maggie's mind caught on the word races. "I remember you calling for volunteers for the event." Narrowing her gaze, she eyed him suspiciously. "Don't tell me you couldn't find anyone else so you volunteered me to race."

Jake glanced at her, his eyes showing his surprise.

"Maggie, the only way I would have volunteered *you* to run in a race in your condition is if you were racing a turtle."

Maggie choked on laughter. "You're just full of compliments today, aren't you?"

"Well, *do* you want to run?"

Maggie shook her head. "Of course not."

Jake smiled. "I didn't think so."

She didn't like his smile. "Jake Mathison, what are you smiling about?"

"Not a thing," he replied blandly, so blandly that she knew he was deliberately lying.

"Lying is a sin."

Jake smiled. "That's right."

"So stop lying to me."

Jake's smile widened. "I'm not."

"You're not?" That smug grin made her want to wipe the street with his face. "There's a catch, isn't there?"

Jake shook his head. "I'm just joking, dear."

Maggie's heart thrilled at the endearment, then his words registered. "So what are you smiling at?"

Jake turned onto Main Street and Maggie forgot her question. Yes, indeed, she was too busy gaping at the sight before her to remember what it was she'd asked. "What in the world are all those beds doing in the middle of the street?"

Jake pulled the truck into a parking lot and several members of the church came over and started unloading it. Jake got out, came around and opened her door. "Look at that," she said and pointed, sliding out, forgetting he hadn't answered. "Brass beds, black beds, a fire-engine bed. They have homemade quilts and... Why are those people all walking around in gowns?''

Maggie turned.

Jake smiled and held up a bag. "Surprise," he said.

Dread shot through her. "Surprise what? I don't like surprises." Warily she opened the bag.

"You volunteered to be the passenger in our annual bed races."

Maggie extracted a huge, antiquated pullover gown that tied at the neck and had long sleeves, a round mop cap and... "Leprechaun shoes?"

Incredulously, she looked up at him.

Jake smiled. "I knew you'd enjoy it. Besides," he added when she didn't say anything, "I got to wear this outfit last year and have no desire to wear it again."

Maggie didn't know what to do. Something she thought long dead surfaced, and she actually laughed at being duped so easily. "You are awful," she said on a gurgle as chuckles finally broke forth.

Tenderly he reached up and cupped her cheek. "I'll be awful or anything else if it'll get you to laugh again like that Maggie-May."

Maggie's laughter died, her gaze taking in Jake's features, the gentleness of his touch, the patience in his eyes.

"There you are, Maggie!"

Elizabeth Jefferson broke the spell. With a child perched on her hip, Elizabeth said coming to a stop beside them, "I had heard you volunteered for this. I just wanted to make sure Jake here wasn't coercing you into it. Jennifer is convinced Jake threatened to cook for you or some other disastrous feat if you don't do it.''

Maggie smiled at her and the man coming up behind her, toting a child, also.

"Hey," Jake said amiably. "My cooking isn't that bad."

Though he joked with Rand and Elizabeth, Maggie could still see something in his eyes. She wasn't sure what, wasn't even sure she wanted to know, but she refused to back out on him after she'd agreed.

"He didn't coerce me at all. He only had to ask."

"Oh, no," Elizabeth groaned. "You'd better learn quick to change that tune or he'll have you doing all kinds of wonderful chores."

Maggie smiled at Elizabeth, taking her ribbing good-naturedly. "That's what I'm paid for, to do chores," she quipped, and set to work getting the voluminous gown over her head.

She felt a pair of hands helping her and knew that it was Jake assisting her. A small shiver passed through her, one both good and bad. "Do you want to tell me just how this works?"

The gown fell down around her shoulders, and she reached up to tie it.

"He didn't tell you?"

Maggie glanced up at Elizabeth. "No." She eyed Jake suspiciously. "He didn't."

Elizabeth's peal of laughter attracted attention from those around her.

"Elizabeth," Rand warned. He smiled sweetly at Maggie. "You'll have to forgive my wife. From what

I understand, she got stuck with this three years ago. And if I understand correctly, it was in the same way you did."

Jake smiled and shrugged. "I love volunteers."

Maggie shook her head. "No one is answering my question."

Just then a voice came over a loudspeaker.

"Come on," Jake said, handing Maggie her green shoes. "We're second in line."

"We'll be rooting for you at the sideline," Elizabeth said.

Rand slipped his arm around Elizabeth and nodded, then turned his wife and led her off.

"You are making me very nervous, Jake Mathison."

Jake touched her back, sending shivers down her spine. "I'd never do anything to hurt you, Maggie."

For some reason, Maggie believed that. He led her through the mingling people and various beds to a blue painted metal bed that had pink stripes encircling the poles. "These colors are awful."

Jake chuckled. "It stands out from the others."

"I'll say it does."

"Come on. Hop up on the bed."

Maggie gaped. "You're kidding me. You expect me to climb up on that?"

Jake grinned. "You sit on it, with or without the sheets pulled over you—that part doesn't matter. Hold on to the bars, and then we push you down Main Street here to city hall. Whoever has the fastest time wins."

"You mean they actually time you?" Maggie was

having a very hard time believing this. "Are you sure it's safe?"

Jake chuckled and patted the bed. "Come on, Maggie."

Reach out, in little steps, one at a time to trust, a voice whispered to her. Maggie hesitated for a moment more before finally deciding to go ahead and try it.

Awkwardly she clambered up on the bed. Several people were there to help push. Tyler—she recognized him—came up and smiled. "You can either sit up and grasp the bars behind you or lie down and grasp the ones at the foot of the bed. Your choice."

Maggie chuckled nervously. "I think I'd rather sit up."

Tyler nodded. "It's actually quite…invigorating."

Maggie's eyes widened. "You have done this?"

Tyler chuckled. "Four years ago."

"What does he do? Wait until someone new comes to the church and grab them?"

A slow smile curved Tyler's lips, and Maggie gaped at how handsome he was when he did that. He nodded.

"You're kidding."

"Nope. That's how he got me. That's how he got Elizabeth. That's how he got two other people. No one thought, with you in your condition, he'd ask you. Should have guessed, though."

Just then a shot sounded, and Maggie saw the bed in front of them shoot forward. That was the only word for it. Shoot—as in a rocket. "They're going fast."

"The speeds get up to almost thirty miles an hour."

Maggie watched as the team pushed until they got to where the street sloped downward. The two people on the back jumped on the back railing. "Oh, my."

Maggie heard the cheering of the crowd, the announcer talking over the voices; saw the people pointing and clapping, the excited faces, the laughter.

"Okay, it's our turn. Hold on."

Maggie felt the warm hand on her shoulder, but it didn't change her opinion. "I'm going to die."

Jake chuckled. "That's the spirit."

"Nothing shakes you."

"Ask me that another time."

The bed jerked as it rolled forward. The vibration of the asphalt through the wheels on the bottom of the bed ran up her spine. There was a click and jerk as the bed rolled over what felt like a crack the size of New Orleans but was certainly no bigger than her finger.

Maggie had to wonder if she was going to be shaken apart going down this slight decline.

The six people from church all swarmed into place, taking what she thought of as a runner's stance. "Ready, Maggie-May?" Jake called.

The gun exploded.

"No!" she yelled, and they took off.

The wind hit Maggie's face, stealing her breath. The cap ripped from her head. Faces of people flew past, and the entire bed felt as though it were flying.

Voices shouted encouragement; cheers echoed in

her ears. She was almost certain she heard Elizabeth shouting her name. The shock faded and she relaxed.

Tyler was right. This was exhilarating. When was the last time she'd done anything that had been considered fun...though she wasn't sure if she would call this fun. She still had to reach the finish line.

A huge bump jarred her, and her hands tightened spasmodically on the bars. Then the bed flew past the concession stand and announcer's podium and they were at the end of their race.

The bed jolted again, jarring her as the six men and women brought it to a stop.

Maggie gasped for breath. She looked around and saw the others gasping and laughing and leaning on the bed. Maggie couldn't resist the urge. She giggled.

Jake appeared at her side, wiping a hand over his forehead, breathing harsh, his face flushed. "Well?"

Maggie knew what he was asking. She grinned like a fool. "It was wonderful!"

Jake reached out for her hand.

Maggie met his eyes. The sounds of cheering, the drone of the voice on the loudspeaker, even the sound of the wind, seemed to fade as she stared at Jake.

Maggie placed her hand in his.

Jake smiled tenderly and tugged.

Maggie flipped her feet around and slid off the bed.

Jake continued to hold her hand, his smile fading as he stared.

"One step at a time, Maggie-May. One step at a time."

Maggie heard the echo of her heart only moments before and nodded numbly.

Slowly the voices returned; the wind whipping at her hair forced her to reach up and push it back. The others who all came running up to congratulate them had to be answered.

Jake finally released her hand. "What say we go have some fun?"

Maggie smiled. "I think I've had more fun just now than I had expected to have the rest of my life."

Jake grinned. "But, Maggie, my darling, the fun has just begun. It only gets better from here on out."

Seeing the mischievous glint in his eyes, Maggie fervently hoped he was right.

Chapter Twelve

"I really appreciate this. Shirley used to do this all the time. I wasn't sure you'd feel up to it."

Maggie listened to Jake's voice in the other room as she tied the huge white bow at her neck.

Ugh.

It was her first maternity suit, and the bow looked like something a two-year-old would wear.

The skirt was straight, hitting just above her knees, and the top flared out over her enlarged abdomen, falling midway down her thighs. It was navy blue, with white piping and large cloth-covered buttons.

"That's what you hired me for," Maggie said practically. "It's part of my job."

"Ah yes, your job." She heard Jake chuckle. Oh, how she liked the sweet rich sound of his voice. "Of course."

Maggie came out of the bedroom into the living room, where Jake stood. She sidestepped Kathryn and then leaned down to pet her. "That's a good girl, Captain Kat. You're doing just fine."

The cat made an awful sound and then wound her way around Maggie's legs before going into the kitchen toward her food.

Jake sneezed.

Maggie sighed. "You ought to go outside, where the cat won't bother you."

"That cat isn't bothering me."

Maggie shook her head disbelievingly. "Very well. The cat isn't bothering you."

After going into the kitchen, she pulled out two plates, bowls and silverware and set them on the table. Quickly she made oatmeal and toast.

"Let me help you, since you invited me to join you," Jake said, coming in and pulling two glasses out of the cabinet.

He took them to the table.

"I'd like milk, please," Maggie said, as he strode to the refrigerator.

Jake pulled open the door and looked inside. "I'll have milk, too."

Strolling back over to the table, he smiled. Maggie wondered what had changed in Jake. He'd been so solicitous to her lately, so gentle and caring.

Her mind drifted back to the bed races two weeks earlier and the look they had shared. Something had changed that day, tilted, throwing her world off-kilter.

Maggie couldn't put her finger on it, but ever since then she'd seen Jake differently, wanted more than she should, desired what she knew she'd never be allowed.

Yet she knew Jake had changed, too. At the office he held himself a bit more distant, though he did spend more time talking to her coming and going from the house. He was also much more careful about coming into her house on errands now, sending Jennifer, instead.

She missed him dropping by. It had thrilled her this morning when he'd stopped by to pick her up a little early, and she'd found out he hadn't had breakfast yet.

Mentally berating herself, she finished setting the table and took her seat.

Jake said a prayer and then Maggie opened her eyes and picked up her spoon.

Nervously, she watched Jake.

"Mmm, this is good."

Though she'd wanted him to like it, she suddenly felt ridiculous. "It's only oatmeal."

She spooned sugar and butter into her oatmeal and mixed it up.

"But I don't cook oatmeal."

Maggie paused with the spoon halfway to her mouth. "You don't cook oatmeal?"

Jake shook his head, taking another bite. He made an *mmm* sound again. "I use the little packets when I have oatmeal. Normally if I cook something for breakfast it's grits."

Maggie chuckled, watching him eat. He was gorgeous even when he ate. A hint of dark along his cheek showed that he would need to shave again that afternoon. His strong jaw worked and his Adam's apple moved when he swallowed.

A sudden dimple appeared in his right cheek. Maggie looked up to meet his eyes, and flushed. "You should be eating, Maggie."

"I am," she mumbled, and shoved the spoon in her mouth.

"So Maggie, tell me, how is the job working out?"

Jake smiled, amused, as Maggie kept her eyes on her bowl and ate. It cheered him to know she wasn't as immune to him as he'd thought. Two weeks ago at the fair, something had happened that had knocked him off his feet. He wasn't sure what. He did know it suddenly didn't matter to him whose child she carried. He wanted her.

She fascinated him like no other woman. In church on Sundays, he found himself watching her worship and the joy on her face. Yet in the world she was so alone.

Jake shared something with her there. He loved God, had a close relationship with Him, closer than any friend. In church he had friends and people he visited, but he still felt alone in some way. Incomplete. There was more he was missing.

Jake decided it was a helpmate, someone to share with, someone whom he could talk to, dream with, be with.

"Tell me your dreams, Maggie."

Maggie almost choked. Jake frowned and reached over, patting her on the back.

"My dreams?" she gasped, wheezing, her eyes tearing.

Concerned, Jake leaned forward to pat her again.

"Please, you'll knock the vertebrae out of alignment if you whack any harder."

Jake chuckled and sat back. "Sorry."

Maggie dabbed at her mouth and sat back. "No problem."

Jake took a sip of his drink. "I didn't mean to shock you."

"I wasn't shocked, exactly. I guess, well, no one thinks I have dreams anymore. I mean, well, not after..." Maggie motioned to her stomach.

She looked so awkward, as she said that. "Everyone has dreams," he said softly, silently asking God to help him through this. Why had he brought this up? Or maybe, just maybe, Maggie did need to talk, to remember, to find her dreams again.

"My dreams..." Maggie took a sip of her milk and another bite of her cereal, before answering. "I wanted to work in my family's business, I suppose."

"And?" he prodded, seeing the odd look in her eye as she stirred absently at the bit of cereal left.

"And I suppose I was like any other girl. I wanted a family—husband, children, a white house with a fence and happily ever after. I wanted someone whom I could love and who would love me back."

Maggie continued to stir, not looking up or saying anything else.

"I've always wanted the center." Jake shared his own dream in this quiet time. Though he'd never revealed much about his life, now he felt he could. It felt—right. "I basically grew up on the streets. Drugs, violence, you name it. I saw my brother killed. Had it not been for someone who cared, I'd probably be dead right now. However, I swore the day I gave my heart to God that I wouldn't stop until I had a center here in the city for kids to go to as a safe place, a refuge. The center has always been my only goal."

Jake paused, glancing at Maggie, who still wasn't looking at him. "It wasn't until…lately, that I started thinking I might want more."

Maggie lifted her eyes and met his gaze. She opened her mouth to reply—or ask a question. He wasn't sure, and never would be because of one blasted obstacle to perfect peace.

"Mmmeeeoooowwwrrrr…"

Claws dug into his leg.

"Ouch!" Jake jumped, shooting back in his chair and upending it in his haste to get loose from the cat.

"Oh, dear!" Maggie gasped, and shoved back, going for the cat, which was still hanging on to Jake's pant leg.

The cat hissed.

Jake stumbled and went down, sprawling.

Captain Kat ran.

"Are you all right?" Maggie moved over to Jake.

Jake sneezed, then looked up from where he lay on the floor. "It only hurts when I laugh." Slowly he gave her a somewhat pain-filled lopsided smile.

Maggie chuckled. "You are ridiculous."

She reached for him, and he shot her a warning look. "Don't even think about it. You'd strain your back."

Jake shoved up and stood, lifting the chair back up. He grabbed his bowl, rinsed it out and then stuck it in the dishwasher.

Maggie cleared the table and finished loading the dishwasher before washing her hands.

"You really should have that cat declawed."

Maggie frowned at him, then went into the living room and grabbed her purse, notebook and files.

"You sure you feel up to this? You're not too tired?"

Maggie sighed loudly. "You've been asking me that for over two weeks now."

Jake smiled and nodded. "If you hadn't pushed yourself so hard at the city celebration and gotten sick, then I wouldn't be asking you."

Maggie scowled and went to the door, digging her keys out of her purse as she did. The clicking of her heels was loud on the hardwood floor. Run, her mind told her. Get away. Get out of the kitchen, out of the house, where there's more space.

She felt sensitive, unsure after sharing her dreams with Jake. What in the world had possessed her to tell Jake what she wanted?

Maggie strode to Jake's car. That smile of his, his touch, that look that had been driving her crazy for two weeks. He was making her feel things she'd thought dead, and she didn't like it one bit.

She had vowed to survive, make it through this situation she was in. Suddenly finding herself attracted to a man, and one who touched her on some deeper level, didn't encourage her.

Jake placed a strong yet gentle hand on the small of Maggie's back. Softly, next to her ear, he whispered, "Maggie-May, did I tell you that you look wonderful today?"

Maggie turned, opened her mouth to call him on the lie, and promptly forgot what she was going to say. Jake's eyes were serious. There was no laughter in them. Only tenderness.

Maggie saw reflected in them something she felt in her own heart: temptation.

She tried again to say something to him, but her voice came out in a small quaver as she spoke words she'd never thought to admit to anyone. "I'm scared."

Jake slid his hand around to her waist and rested it there on her side. "Me, too."

A hot humid breeze wafted through the air, carrying the spicy scent of Jake's aftershave to her. Maggie inhaled, leaning forward slightly, allowing herself to enjoy the temporary feel of his hand at her waist. "Why?"

She wasn't sure he'd heard her whisper until he leaned forward and responded, "Because I don't want to see you hurt—again."

"You won't hurt me."

"I won't hurt you," he agreed, his other hand coming up and brushing a piece of hair from her face.

"But I might hurt you," she replied.

The draw of his hand on her cheek was irresistible. Maggie had yearned so long for the touch of another human being. For months now, she'd lived in a void, without touch or companionship. Jake and others had offered companionship. But the touch...

Maggie luxuriated in the rough feel of his hand against her cheek. Just for a moment, what could it hurt to give in, enjoy...

Maggie sighed.

"Oh, Maggie," Jake murmured. "If this is hurt, I'll gladly suffer."

Jake leaned forward and touched his lips to hers in a gentle, yet consuming kiss.

Maggie reeled. Her breath left in a rush. Pleasure filled her, pleasure and...fear.

She jerked back, her breathing hard. Her mind swirled with old and new sensations, until she finally looked up and met Jake's eyes.

Concern and something else shone in them. Maggie averted her gaze.

"Should I apologize?" Jake asked softly.

"No!" Maggie turned toward the car. "Not at all. I—I wanted it, too."

Why she admitted that she wasn't sure. But it was the truth.

Jake opened the car door for her, and Maggie climbed in.

He walked around the front of the vehicle, then slid behind the wheel. The sound of his door closing was loud. The engine turned over, and his hand went to the back of the seat as he looked over his shoulder to back out.

"You still have that shopping list Jennifer mentioned?"

Whatever Maggie had expected, it hadn't been that. "Yes. I do."

Jake nodded. "Good. After the meeting, we'll go shopping. How does that sound?"

Maggie thought it sounded like a long time in

Jake's company. She wasn't sure if that was good or bad. So instead of answering, she said, "Thank you."

"It's no problem."

The car turned, and they were headed into Baton Rouge.

Maggie decided it was going to be a very long drive.

Chapter Thirteen

"We're here."

Maggie groggily opened her eyes and looked around. "Wha—?"

The deep sound of Jake's sweet voice echoed in the car. "You fell asleep, Maggie."

"I what? I did not." Maggie was appalled. She never slept in the car.

"I didn't mean to," she apologized.

Jake chuckled. "Then the baby must have decided you needed it. Don't worry. You almost made it all the way to the city limits before sleeping."

Maggie's cheeks heated. "I've been out that long?"

Jake nodded. He slipped from the car and came around to open her door. "Have you been having trouble resting?"

Maggie shrugged. "Only intermittently. I have an occasional nightmare."

Maggie scooted to the edge of her seat and then stood. Automatically, she reached up to cover her head with a hand against the misty rain that fell.

"Is this the place?" she asked to change the subject from her sleeping habits and nightmares.

Maggie looked at the hotel where they were meeting and realized it was one she had sometimes reserved for her parents when they had people from out of town coming in and were going to conduct several meetings. The hotel had wonderful accommodations and great conference rooms. The food wasn't bad, but the small Mexican restaurant next to it was great.

Maggie checked her folders, the notebook and then her purse before following Jake into the hotel. "You should have wakened me."

"You looked tired, Maggie. Don't be embarrassed that you took a short nap. I can't tell you how many times Shirley caught me snoozing in my office."

Maggie didn't like being vulnerable, and sleeping made her vulnerable. Once inside she crossed the maroon carpet with Jake, doing her best to look like a professional assistant instead of a pregnant lady who'd just had a nap. "Here are the files you needed in regard to the plans you wanted."

Jake took the file folder from her and thumbed through it. Maggie flipped her notebook open and slipped her pen in the rings, following Jake around the corner.

"Here we are," he said, going toward one of the conference rooms.

Maggie heard Jake, but her eyes were on the water

fountain just outside the doors. "I'll be right there," she said, and headed toward the relief.

"I'll be just inside."

"Okay." Maggie went over to relieve her thirst. Cool refreshing water filled her mouth, reviving her.

"Jake!"

She heard the male voice and Jake's good-natured response. The murmur of other voices reached her, and she still drank. After her fourth sip she forced herself to stand and take a deep breath. How long had it been since she'd done work like this? Surely not since working for her parents.

She checked her papers again and then went to the door.

Perhaps fifteen or twenty people stood around in groups, talking. All wore different styles of dress, from casual to three-piece suits. The room was set up with three tables in a U shape. Small plates and snacks were laid out on them.

No wonder Jake hadn't eaten. He probably knew there would be coffee and croissants.

Maggie should have known. If she hadn't been rattled by Jake's showing up so early, it would have come back to her. She searched the room with her eyes until she found Jake. He stood so at ease as he smiled and talked. She could see him through some people standing around him.

Their eyes met and Jake lifted a hand…just as the other person moved.

Maggie's smile disappeared. The blood drained from her face. Black dots appeared before her eyes, and the room swam.

The murmur of voices sounded like a sudden roar. Maggie turned and stumbled from the room.

Blindly she reached out until she found the wall. Maggie gripped at it, leaning heavily against its cool support against her left cheek.

It couldn't be. She couldn't believe what she saw. That couldn't have been...

Strong arms slipped around her, pulling her back against a firm steady body. Maggie jerked, gasping, opening her mouth to scream, when the sweet warm voice of Jake reached her.

"Maggie? What is it? Are you okay?"

Panic left. Relief filled her and she sagged against him, her legs turning to jelly.

Jake turned slightly. An arm slipped under her legs and he lifted her.

"No, Jake, I—" she protested as he lifted her.

"Shh. You look faint."

Maggie didn't argue the fact. She did feel faint. "Please, I don't want them to see me," she whispered weakly, grabbing at his shoulders.

Jake, who had started toward the lobby, turned and walked in the direction of the service elevators and other conference rooms, instead. Jake finally lowered her to the soft leather cushions of a nearby sofa. Only when he removed his arms from under her thighs and she felt the brush of her folders did she realize she must have dropped her supplies.

Oxygen returned to her brain and the fog slowly cleared. When she focused clearly again it was to see Jake sitting on the couch next to her, one of her hands clasped in his as he leaned over her.

"Do you need a doctor?"

"No! I guess not getting enough sleep caught up with me."

Jake gave her a look of skepticism. But thankfully he didn't call her on the lie. "Let me get the car and I'll take you home."

"Oh, no, Jake. Your meeting!" Maggie tried to struggle up, but Jake's hand on her shoulder held her down.

"I only have some plans to present. Tyler is here. I'll have him get everything and run the meeting for me. But I'm taking you home."

Maggie felt miserable that Jake was going to miss his meeting, but she was relieved to get out of there. Her heart was still racing, and she wasn't sure if breakfast was going to stay down.

Jake stood and dug through her files, pulling out what he needed. "You don't move. I'll be right back."

"Please, don't tell anyone about...me."

Jake paused, gave her a curious look, then nodded. "If that's what you want."

"It is." Jake started to turn away, but she stopped him. "Wait." Maggie leaned over and grabbed her purse. She dug in it, retrieving a tape recorder. "If you can get Tyler to record the meeting, I'll be glad to transcribe the tape later."

"Great."

He took the cassette player. When their fingers touched, he paused studying her. He opened his mouth, then closed it before saying, "I'm here for you."

Maggie saw the curiosity and concern in Jake's face. She wanted to reach out, to tell him everything, but she couldn't. Right now all she wanted to do was curl up and hide. "I know," she whispered.

"So is God."

"I know," she repeated.

At last, she pulled her hand from under his, leaving the recorder in his grip, and lay back against the soft leather cushions of the camel-colored couch.

As soon as Jake was out of sight, a trembling started deep down inside her. Old fears, rages, inadequacies, shame, all threatened to overwhelm her. She hadn't expected to see *him* ever again. Oh, she should have known. But in a town of over 500,000 what were the chances of seeing *him*, especially since she didn't travel in those circles anymore? And *he* had been standing there with her parents.

Maggie shuddered and wrapped her arms around herself. Slowly she rocked back and forth, trying to stop the memories. A shadow crossed over her but she didn't really register it until a gentle hand touched her shoulder.

"Jake." The whisper slipped involuntarily past her lips. Warm arms slipped around her, pulling her close. "It'll be okay."

Maggie shook her head. She couldn't talk about it. If she did, she'd fall to pieces.

He stroked her back. As he did this, Maggie felt the shudders fade. Eventually, she relaxed against him. He shifted, picked up the files and her purse, handing them to her before scooping her up.

"I can walk, Jake," she protested.

"I'm sure you can. But just let me do this. You still look too pale."

Because her legs still wobbled like pudding she didn't argue. She did note she and Jake weren't going the same way they had come. "Where are you taking me?"

"I had one of the bellhops pull the car around to a side entrance that was closer."

Maggie sagged against him in relief. "Thank you."

In what seemed like hours but was probably less than two minutes, Jake was tucking her into the car. He quickly slid in behind the wheel and left without a backward glance.

All was quiet as he pulled onto the interstate and into Baton Rouge morning traffic. He didn't ask for an explanation or ply her with questions; he simply drove.

Maggie couldn't stand it.

"It looks like the rain has stopped."

"Rainy season. Hurricane season." Jake shrugged.

"I'm sorry," she finally whispered.

Jake changed lanes before glancing over at her, concerned. "Maggie, you have nothing to apologize for. You wanted to leave so we left. Even if you hadn't been sick, we'd have left if you needed to. I'd like to know what's going on—I'll admit that. But if you don't want to tell me, I won't demand it."

Maggie wanted to confess it all to him. She opened her mouth, but the crushing weight of fear and shame enclosed her in a web, making speech impossible.

Maggie fell back against the seat and turned her head, staring out the window into the distance.

Jake's hand groped and found hers. His clasp felt warm against her own clammy fingers. But what really radiated warmth through her was when he began to pray. Maggie's heart expanded, fluttering at his words. He prayed for her joy, her day, his day, all kinds of simple everyday things, as well as for her fear. Jake continued to hold her hand and praise God for the things He had bestowed on them, the joys He gave them in the world, and on and on, until Maggie felt a peace invade the car, and her heart.

Slowly the ice within her melted, and the fear left. Jake knew that, too, for he squeezed her hand tightly, then released it.

Looking around, Maggie realized they were home. "Thank you, Jake."

Jake simply nodded.

Maggie waited until the car stopped and climbed out. She smoothed her skirt, gathered up her papers and purse, then headed toward the house.

"You didn't let me open your door, Maggie-May."

Maggie heard him following and silently admitted how very nice that nickname suddenly sounded on his lips and how much it meant to walk her to her door. "I thought you might try to make the last part of the meeting and didn't want to delay you."

Jake cocked his head to the side, eyeing her strangely. "Like I said, Tyler or Gage can handle it. Besides, I think there was mention of a grocery list earlier?"

Maggie shook her head. "It can wait. I can go later."

"You sure you don't want me to run the errands for you? Milk, bread, anything?"

"No. Really. I'll manage."

Jake walked her up to the porch and watched as she inserted the key in the lock. "By the way, Maggie, I've thought about this and I think it might be better if Jennifer helped me with the meetings. If she takes a tape recorder, then it won't be necessary for you to go."

Maggie bristled. "It's part of my job."

"Do you really want to go?"

Jake asked it softly. The sound ran through her.

"No," she finally whispered, holding on to the door. "I can't go. I shouldn't even stay here. This job is wrong. If I can't do the entire job, you should find someone who can."

Jake didn't hesitate but stepped forward and pulled Maggie into his arms. "I want you in the job, Maggie-May. Only you."

"You don't understand, Jake." Maggie slipped her arms around him, allowing some of his strength and warmth to flow into her. "Things always go wrong with me. It's only a matter of time...."

Jake rocked her, his arms like steel as they held her close. Maggie dimly wondered when their relationship had developed to hugging and holding but decided she didn't mind so she wasn't going to complain.

"Trust God, Maggie. You just believe in Him and put your trust there."

"I want to." And she did. But she just knew, if she stayed, things would eventually go wrong. If her parents had seen her today, there would be problems. They were so ashamed of her *condition*. They would raise the roof until she couldn't face Jake or he fired her.

She didn't want that.

"Just keep trying. That's all you have to do."

Maggie leaned back, lifting her gaze to him.

Jake leaned down giving her time to pull back.

She didn't.

Their lips met. No fear assailed her, only a relief and joy that despite everything that had happened, he still cared.

The baby moved, kicked, and Jake pulled back. Surprise curved his face into astonishment as he looked down. He reached out, then hesitated.

Maggie gently captured his hand and placed it on the moving child.

"Wow," Jake murmured, looking up in awe. "Is the baby always this active?"

Maggie shook her head. "On and off."

Tears filled and overflowed her eyes. Jake frowned and brushed first at one trail and then the other. "It doesn't hurt, does it? Rand never said that Elizabeth was in any pain."

Maggie chuckled and gave Jake a watery smile. "No, it doesn't hurt. It's just that until recently the child wasn't even real to me. You're the first person to share anything like this."

Maggie stepped back and wrapped her arms around herself. Jake hated seeing her look so vulnerable. He wanted to reach out and haul her back into his arms and tell her he'd not let anything happen to her. But if his suspicions were correct, his Maggie had already been through enough to last anyone more than a lifetime.

"I'm not even sure if I'm going to keep this baby."

Stunned, Jake stared. She just looked so *motherly* to him, so made for children. "It's your choice, Maggie. Just pray, seek God, see how He would lead you in this. And if you decide to give the baby up, I know a couple of good families who would be overjoyed to adopt a child."

Maggie nodded and reached for the door.

"For what it's worth, I think you'd make a good mother."

Maggie paused. "No, I don't think so."

"You were great with those kids on Saturday. Eddie is more than half in love with you. Do you know he's called the church twice this week to see if you've had the baby yet?"

Astonished, Maggie said, "But I still have a month to go...."

Jake chuckled. "He doesn't care. He's just checking up on you. And there is a tenderness in you, a softness. It's tempered with the pain of going through the fire, but it's there, strong, steady, a strength to help a child going through his or her own problems."

Maggie's hand trembled. Jake barely resisted the urge to reach out and touch it. "You might not see that strength now, but one day, you're going to see, Maggie-May, how God has sustained you through this. Pray. I'll be here to help."

Maggie nodded, and without turning went into her house.

Jake walked back down the steps thinking of this morning's events. *Oh, Father, why did you bring her into my life? Now, right when I'm about to see my dream, the dream of my entire life realized?*

Jake remembered the fear and shock in her eyes when she'd looked at him in that room. What had she seen to scare her so badly? He was dying to know but understood that if he was meant to know, Maggie would share it eventually.

Amused exasperation, Jake groaned. "Why now?"

Perhaps God was telling him there was something more for him than what he had right now.

And he hoped that the something more was the woman he'd just left at the front door of the white clapboard house.

Chapter Fourteen

"I don't want no pizza unless it's Mr. Peeper's pizza."

Maggie chuckled. "Mr. Peeper's?" She glanced down at Eddie, who was walking, chin thrust out, shoulders back, as though he owned the whole world.

"Mr. Peeper's is a new place in town," Jake explained.

"Ah, I see." Maggie nodded wisely and smiled back down at Eddie. "I guess Fair and Fun is out then." Maggie sighed. "And I was so looking forward to the rides."

Eddie's eyes lit up, before he forced the excitement away. "You're preggo. How you gonna ride those rides?"

Maggie gasped. "Well, I certainly may be pregnant, but that doesn't mean I have to give up all my fun."

Eddie squinted up at her, then nodded. "I guess if

she wants to go there, Pastor Jake, we gotta take her.
You know how pregnant women get. My sister cries
her eyes out when she don't get her way.''

Jake chuckled. ''We certainly don't want that.''

They went over to the car and climbed in. Jake had
explained that occasionally he'd pick up two or three,
even all the kids for something special.

In fifteen minutes they were at the park. Amused,
Maggie watched Eddie scramble out of the car, no
longer the little man of the house but pure child.

''What are we going to do first, Pastor Jake?''

''Well, are you hungry or do you want to ride?''

''Ri—'' Eddie glanced toward Maggie. ''Women
are always hungry.''

Maggie laughed. ''Excuse me, but if I have my
choice, I want to ride the Spider first.''

Eddie's eyes widened, then a big grin split his face.
''You are one cool lady.''

Maggie gaped in surprise as he turned and ran off
toward the entrance.

''You know, Maggie-May, I think I agree with him.
You are one cool lady.'' Jake chuckled and slipped
an arm around her shoulders, hugging her to him. ''I
think you just won a place in Eddie's heart for the
rest of his life.''

Maggie thrilled at the touch, leaning into Jake.
''I'm glad. He's a sweet kid—sometimes.''

''Hey come on, you two. Oh, yuck. You're hugging
her, Pastor Jake.''

Jake released her. ''Yeah, I am.'' He reached out
to where Eddie had run back to them and snagged

him. "And I'm hugging you, too," he said, and put words to action.

"Men don't hug men!" Eddie stated stoutly, squirming to get away, but not too hard.

"Well, I'm a pastor, so I guess I can," Jake said, chuckling and then releasing him. "Now, come on, let's go."

Jake reached out and took Maggie's elbow before sliding his hand down to her hand.

"Do you think you should..." Maggie eyed their hands.

"Unless you mind," Jake said.

Indecision warred on her face.

"Maggie, I'm only holding your hand. Would it bother you if it was any other man?"

Old memories rose, haunting her. She wanted to say yes. Yes, it would. That only Jake could hold her hand without making her squirm. "I don't mind," she said, instead. Then she smiled.

Jake felt something expand in his chest at that smile. "Come on, let's go have fun."

"I hope I'm really up to this. It's been ages since I've been on any rides."

Jake pulled out his wallet, releasing Maggie's hand to pay for three passes. "Just how long is that?" he queried, as he waited while the attendant put a bracelet on each of their wrists.

Jake glanced up just in time to see a blank stare on Maggie's face. "Twenty years?" Maggie said, her face scrunching up as she tried to remember if that was correct.

Jake shook his head. Eddie jumped in before Jake could reply, "You're *that* old?"

Jake smothered a smile.

"Yes, I'm *that* old, Eddie."

"You sure you should ride the rides, then?"

Eddie's wide-eyed stare told Jake the kid was serious about his question. "Uh, one thing to learn, Eddie, is never to question a woman about her age."

Maggie shot Eddie a militant look. "We'll just have to see who gives out first. Now, which way to the Spider?"

Eddie looked as if he had grave reservations. However, he led Jake and Maggie over to it. By the time he reached it all worry was gone and only excitement showed.

"Come on, let's go." He reached back, grabbed Maggie's hand and dragged her forward.

Maggie grinned like an unsure kid who had been told she could walk on air and wanted to believe it but just wasn't sure.

Jake placed a gentle hand at her back. "Come on, Maggie. I'm right behind you."

Maggie hesitated one more moment before giving over. Indecision yielded to firm conviction and she went forward, almost causing Eddie to stumble in his eagerness. They climbed onto the ride with Eddie in the middle, and then slowly it started.

Jake watched Maggie's eyes widen, then she gasped. Concerned, he started to signal the man to stop. Maggie ended his concern with a whoop and laugh as she leaned over and grabbed Eddie's leg.

"Isn't this great!" she cried out over the increasing noise.

"Yeah, cool!" Eddie stuck his little arms up in the air and let loose with a shout.

Maggie imitated him.

Jake shook his head and held on, laughing.

When that ride was over, Maggie led them to another and another, until they had ridden every ride in the park. Then she demanded pizza and bowled at the miniature alleys before shooting in the shooting gallery. She even challenged Eddie to a game of air hockey and played video games with him.

Jake couldn't have been more pleased. Though Maggie feared her pregnancy and had told him she wasn't sure she'd make a good mom, she was proving to him over and over just what type of woman she was.

The way she handled Eddie, even though she had no idea she was doing it. Handing him a napkin, laughing with him, treating him as though he mattered. This showed how much she cared.

Why couldn't she see it?

When Jake noted Eddie's eyes drooping he called an end to the evening. "I think it's time we go. I have to get up early tomorrow." He added the last diplomatically when he saw Eddie about to argue that he wasn't tired.

Eddie subsided. "You got to work," he mumbled, and stood.

Maggie reached out and caught Eddie by the shoulder, pulling him awkwardly up against him. Her whole posture softened when he leaned against her.

Jake helped them both into the car and dropped Eddie at home, tucking him in, then talking for a few minutes with the mother and sister.

Finally they left.

"You look tired, too, Maggie-May."

The comfort of his strong arm around her shoulders encouraged Maggie to relax against him. Warmth and strength radiated from him. Maggie absorbed it, enjoying the strength. When he stopped by the car, she reluctantly stepped away so he could open the door.

Sitting down on the soft seat, she realized suddenly she was very tired.

"Maggie?"

Maggie blinked and glanced over. Jake had climbed into his seat. "Yes."

Jake smiled and touched her cheek. "Sleep. I'll wake you when we get home."

"I'm not that tir..." Maggie trailed off, then scowled. "Fine. I'll close my eyes. Satisfied?"

"Yes."

"Don't look so smug," she warned, closing her eyes as Jake pulled out. "They may be closed, but I'm not asleep."

Maggie walked through the room, her sequined dress glittering brightly under the chandeliers. Though Maggie didn't drink, several people there did, and they all held wineglasses in their hands, laughing and talking.

Maggie searched, looking for her date. Her feet hurt. She was tired. She'd done her duty by her parents and was going home. They had these parties oc-

casionally when her parents helped a great deal with some project.

But three hours was enough for her. Besides, it was Christmas Eve and she wanted to get home. She and Chester had plans to make. She was supposed to go over to his parents tomorrow evening and then they were going to go out and discuss the wedding plans.

May was close. They had to get those invitations sent out. And when everything had quieted down, Chester's mother wanted Maggie to finish up the invitations and get them out before the first.

Again she looked, going into the billiard room and the den and finally toward the dining room.

Finally she saw him. He stood with her parents, laughing. Maggie went over and informed her parents she was going to leave.

Her parents worried. It was raining outside and dangerous. Why not let Chester drive her and they'd see her later?

Maggie agreed. She and Chester left. The cold rain pelted her in the face, causing goose bumps to raise on her arms.

Maggie hugged herself as Chester got the car. Gratefully she accepted his jacket as he helped her into the car.

Voices were distorted as the sound of the car roared in her ears. She saw herself laugh, then Chester laugh and reach over and pat her leg.

The house, looking elongated and dark, came into view and Chester drove up to the door. After coming around, he opened her door and then escorted her in.

When she tried to give him back his jacket, he

shook his head, grabbing the lapels and pulling her forward for a kiss.

Maggie giggled and kissed him, then tried to step back. He walked her backward, teasing her with words and kisses until they were in a side room.

Maggie looked around, panic building in her as she knew what was coming. She tried to reach out to the person in the dream, her own self, and warn her, but she couldn't get there. Chester pushed her down on the couch to give her another kiss...and another...Maggie watched from a camera's view as the scene progressed. She couldn't breathe. She was trapped, the world growing dark...pain...suffocation...she had to scream...to scream...to scream....

"Maggie!"

Maggie jerked up, gasping for breath. Wildly she struck out, whimpering noises rising in her throat.

Hands grabbed at her. Male hands. Strong hands. Her flesh crawled.

"Maggie! Maggie! It's me...Jake."

Dimly Maggie heard the soothing voice. The hands grabbing at her weren't the hands of force but hands that tried to gentle.

Gasping, Maggie looked around wildly and saw... Jake.

Jake fought to keep from getting his eyes scratched out, horrified at the reaction of the woman before him.

"Maggie? Are you okay?"

He watched her heaving as she stared at him, her pupils dilated, her face pale even in the dark car. He stilled. "Maggie, darling, it's okay. It's me, Jake. We're home."

Her eyes lost the wild look and focused on him.

"We're home," he repeated, holding on to her fingers.

Suddenly her hands moved forward, and she was doing the holding.

Jake let her. He waited. Finally she let out a long breath and collapsed against the seat. "Maggie, I'm going to let go of you, just for a minute, okay?"

Her hands tightened. Jake hesitated but decided she would understand once he took action.

Reluctantly, he released her hands, then exited the car and strode around the hood. After pulling open the door, he squatted next to her. When he reached out and touched her, she jumped again.

After only a moment's hesitation, she went into his arms. Jake willingly took her, scooping her up, then shutting the door with his hip.

"Maggie-May, darling, you're trembling like a leaf. Hold on, I'm going to take you inside."

Jake strode across the lawn and up the steps. Fumbling, he managed to get the screen open. "Dig in your purse, Maggie, and get me your keys."

Maggie moved sluggishly, as if caught between the nightmare and reality. Grimly, Jake thought the nightmare was probably reality from the past.

Slowly Maggie fumbled and found her key and shifted to put it in the lock.

Jake prayed silently. He shoved the door open, flipping on a light, and asked God for peace, protection, for His spirit to surround Maggie. He continued to pray all the way into her bedroom, words of comfort and assurance.

"Mmmrrrrroooowww?" Captain Kat lay in the middle of her bed.

When the cat saw Jake her meow turned to a growl. As Captain Kat hopped up, her hair was standing straight up. "That cat is going to be the death of me, Maggie, I swea—achhhooo!"

Jake turned his head, barely missing sneezing on Maggie. Carefully he lowered her to the bed, then sniffled.

He almost landed on top of her when she didn't release his neck. After going down to the edge of the bed, he kept her up against him, holding her, rubbing her back, praying and making soothing noises— smothering his occasional sniffle—until she calmed.

He wanted to ask her. But he felt a check in his spirit. So he simply waited. Finally, softly, in a voice he could barely hear, she confessed.

"I have nightmares occasionally, about...things. I'm sorry you had to witness it."

Knowing he had to let her go at her own pace, he replied, "Don't worry about me witnessing it. I'm simply glad I was here for you."

His heart almost broke when he felt tears wetting his shoulder. He pulled her closer, holding her, trying to give her comfort.

The baby kicked.

And kicked again.

Maggie shifted.

It kicked once more.

"Why is it kicking me like that?"

Maggie's muffled laughter caused him to lean back and look at her.

Red-nosed, watery-eyed, she smiled up at him. "It's got the hiccups."

"You're kidding."

Jake looked down at her stomach, and sure enough, her entire stomach jerked. Fascinated, he watched, waiting, and then it jumped again and finally again. "Doesn't that keep you awake?"

Maggie leaned back against the headboard and smiled wanly. "Yes and no. You learn to sleep through some of it. It's only if the baby gets really bad that you are awakened."

"I see." Without thinking, Jake reached out and touched her stomach. Immediately he jerked back. "I'm sorry—I..."

Maggie took his hand and placed it back on her stomach. He chuckled as he felt the child move, settle, then hiccup again.

"That is hilarious."

"I'll remember that at 2 a.m. in the morning when the baby is doing that, and I'm having to get up because the bouncing keeps making me have to go to the bathroom."

"Oh." Jake grinned. He suddenly realized he was sitting on her bed with her, in the middle of the night, which he felt crossed the line of propriety. And though God knew his heart had been in helping her, now it wasn't. Now it was on the way her red corkscrew curls fell around her face, the way her green eyes sparkled with residual fear as she fought and gained control.

It was on how soft she looked from the living-room light, how maternal she looked with one hand resting on top of his where his rested on her stomach.

It felt too good, too right.

Jake pulled back his hand and stood. "I'll be here for you, Maggie. All you have to do is call. I live only a few hundred yards away. If you don't want to stay alone, perhaps I can call one of the women of the church—maybe Jennifer—to come sleep with you tonight."

The smile faded and shadows resurfaced in her eyes. "No. No, I'll be fine, Jake."

Maggie struggled to get up.

"Stay there."

"I have to lock the door behind you."

Jake conceded she was right. "I don't like you staying alone after that nightmare. Are you sure—"

"I'm sure," she replied.

Jake hesitated, tempted to lean forward and kiss her. A growl came from behind him, raising the hairs on the back of his neck.

He sneezed.

Maggie chuckled. "Kathryn will protect me."

Jake sneezed again and quickly strode to the front door. Stepping out on the porch, he breathed in deeply.

Turning back, he saw Maggie standing by the door, holding the screen, the cat weaving awkwardly around her legs. He leaned forward and kissed her forehead, daring the cat to do anything about it. "Call me, any hour, if you want to talk."

He stepped back.

Maggie looked up at him, and he saw in her eyes emotions he couldn't put a name to. "I will," she whispered.

"Promise?"

"Promise." She nodded.

"Lock the door before I leave."

Maggie nodded, hesitated, then nodded again and pushed the door closed. The resounding click told him the dead bolt had slid home. He heard her give it a jerk and thought he heard a whispered, "Good night."

Reaching out, he touched the screen. *Protect her, Father, while I can't. Keep her safe, because I've decided I'm going to make that woman mine.*

Slowly he turned and walked down the stairs in a daze. Maggie.

His Maggie.

He loved her.

When had it happened?

Jake had no idea. He only knew the feeling was there and it wasn't going away.

Suddenly a grin split his face. *He loved her!*

When he got to the car he hopped in and pulled over to his driveway grinning like an idiot.

He loved her.

And she was pregnant and had been sorely hurt in her past.

Jake frowned, but only for a moment. *God, you are the keeper of our hearts. Heal her heart. Heal her mind. Give me the wisdom on how to help that healing. Show me how to offer her my love without running her off.*

He shut off the engine and got out of his car. Looking back at Maggie's house, he saw she'd left on the light in the living room. *Chase away her demons,* he whispered. *Protect her....*

Then he addressed Maggie. "And get ready, Maggie. This preacher is coming a courting."

With a chuckle, he went into his house, already planning his strategy to win the beautiful angel with eyes the color of clover.

Chapter Fifteen

"Maggie, are you awake?"

Maggie looked up from the couch in the darkened room she was lying in to see Jennifer silhouetted in the harsh lights of the hall. "Yes. Jake just insists I take this hour break every day."

Jennifer chuckled.

Maggie started to swing around and sit up.

"No, stay like that. I just brought you a snack. I thought you might like something small to eat while you rested."

"You guys are spoiling me!" Maggie said this, though she felt special, very very special. "Thank you," she added, reaching for the plate. "Oh, more broccoli."

Jennifer dropped into a chair next to the couch. "Jake doesn't have an assistant pastor. Lucky for you, huh."

"I would think Tyler..."

Maggie had discovered this office only when Jake had told her to start taking a daily break and led her to the room. It had a desk, bare walls, two chairs and a sofa. That was it.

"Tyler will help out, but he's not called to the ministry."

"I see."

"Go on, eat up. It's good for you."

Obediently Maggie munched.

"Jake said you had gone to eating six meals a day."

Maggie scowled. "I'm not surprised he'd gloat. He's been telling me forever to do that."

"One more month, right?"

Maggie nodded. "The first time Jake noticed my ankles were swollen he made me start taking these breaks."

Jennifer giggled. "That man is so besotted with you."

Maggie was glad it was dark so Jennifer couldn't see her flush. "Well, it doesn't matter. Nothing can ever come of it."

It was embarrassing and had her worried that Jake had been looking at her differently for almost a week now. Something had changed the night she'd had the nightmare.

She'd been worried the next day about how he might act. She hadn't expected the looks of interest or extra attention he spent touching her or taking her out. Nor had she realized he was paying such close attention that he'd see her swollen ankles.

"Why do you say that?" Jennifer sounded surprised, shocked.

Was everyone so dense here? For months now she'd walked around on eggshells as people had pretended her pregnancy didn't make a difference. Frustration built and exploded. "Jennifer, I'm pregnant by a man he doesn't even know about. Bad luck seems to follow me. Can you imagine what would happen if I even let myself believe that Jake could really care for me? Eventually I'll have to leave when something happens, when someone starts complaining or gossiping."

"No! Jake would never ask you to leave, Maggie. He cares for you. It's obvious."

Maggie felt a weight settle in on her heart. "He might never ask me, but he'd be relieved. Just like my par—"

Maggie clamped her mouth shut.

Silence fell. Finally, Maggie heard the squeak of leather as Jennifer shifted. "Did I ever tell you how Gage and I met?"

"Jake said he was your pilot."

"Umm-hmm," she said. "That was the most interesting trip I have ever had. Gage was a very bitter man."

"Uh, perhaps…" Maggie began.

"I don't think he'd mind me sharing this with you," Jennifer said matter-of-factly. "Many people in the church know most of the story. Anyway, he got home just in time to find out his fiancée was marrying someone while he was still engaged to her. He had to come home for his mother's funeral. You see, the entire time he had been in Korea—he was a soldier stationed there for a short tour—his mother had been lying to him, telling him everything was okay. Gage stopped trusting women completely. He was so hurt and bitter and believed nothing could be believed. He threw himself into his business. That was all that mattered. Nothing else. He was going to make his business a success—which he has. But at that time it was still shaky.''

Jennifer shifted again in the quiet room. ''Then here I come. I tend to be...optimistic. And Gage was a pessimist. He found guns in crates we were delivering to San Gabriel for a relief mission and he was certain I knew about them. But on a deeper level, as we trekked through the jungle, he had to deal with his very fears—that if he opened up, he was going to be betrayed again. He fought it, dragging me toward the closest city, determined to get rid of me so he wouldn't have to face his feelings.

''The only thing he forgot in that equation is that if God wants you to deal with something, He's going to see that you do. I think Gage getting temporarily blinded, the soldiers capturing us, the rebels robbing us, were all to keep us out there until we worked through things God wanted changed in our hearts.''

Maggie shook, Jennifer's story going straight to her heart. *But why, Father? Why am I going through this? Are you trying to teach me something? Am I running from something?*

Maggie didn't want an answer because she knew what she was running from. Memories and the pain of being hurt again. Not physically but emotionally.

Tears filled her eyes. As much as she wanted to believe what Jennifer was saying, she just couldn't open up and trust Jake completely. She just couldn't. He was a good man. But when things went wrong, she wasn't going to be able to stand there and watch him suffer for her mistakes, the sorrow she would bring to him.

Trust Me.

The soft sweet voice sent chills down her arms. She shivered. *I'm trying.*

Trust Me, the voice repeated.

I—I—can't.

"Trust Him, Maggie. Let Him heal your heart. Just step out and believe that He will take care of everything." Jennifer stood. "I have to get back to those adorable little rug rats. I'll send someone by for the plate later."

"Thank you." Maggie watched Jennifer leave. Touching her stomach, she whispered, *How, Father? How can I put it all behind me? How can I trust and forget and go on? I don't even know if I can keep the baby yet? How can I heal if I haven't even made that decision?*

Maggie realized that healing and trust were going hand in hand. Despite her feelings for Jake, it could never be because of her bitterness and anger. What type of wife would she make? How could she support him in his ministry, and as a man, when she was unable to get over her own hurts?

Wearily pushing up, she went back to the office to work and think on what Jennifer had said.

* * *

The pounding on the door brought Maggie up. Heart racing, she grabbed for her robe and waddled through the house.

"Maggie! Maggie, it's me, Jake!"

Maggie jerked open the door, still pulling on her robe. When she saw Jake's face, she knew something had happened. "What is it?" She squinted. "It's after midnight. Are you okay? Is it my parents?"

"It's Eddie. He's been shot."

Maggie gasped. "What happened?" She rushed back into her room, and started pulling on clothes as fast as she could.

"Gang. Something like that. I didn't get the entire story from his sister. She was crying. He's at the hospital. I thought you'd want to go with me."

Maggie's heart beat loudly as she thought of the cute kid, and couldn't believe what Jake was telling her. "Eddie. Shot." She shook her head.

After grabbing her shoes and socks, she strode into the room where Jake was waiting. He helped her down the stairs, his face etched in harsh lines.

"What do you know?" Maggie asked, climbing into the car. Once in the car she realized she couldn't get her socks on, so she dropped them and slipped on just her shoes.

"There was a fight of some sort. Eddie got in the middle. A gun went off. That's it. Elaina wasn't making much sense at the time. Her mama was in with Eddie, evidently. Big wreck or something in town so they brought him up here to the hospital instead of one of the other ones."

Jake sped along down the highway before turning

in to the local hospital. Maggie was thankful it was so close. Any farther, she would have expired from worry.

Jake let her out and went to park the car.

When she entered, she saw the sister. Mother and daughter sat weeping, holding each other. A large group of friends or relatives stood around, talking and weeping…waiting for news, she assumed. Not knowing what else to do, Maggie started toward them.

Relief flooded her when Jake came in. Touching her back, he led her forward. Elaina saw them first. With a loud cry she came toward Jake. Jake didn't hesitate but opened his arms and enfolded her in a hug. Looking at the mother, he asked, "What news?"

A woman sitting next to a middle-aged woman glanced up and said, "They got him back there now. We haven't heard anything yet."

Jake nodded. The mother, eyes red and swollen, looked up. "They shot my baby," she cried. "Came right in my house and tried to shoot Elaina. Eddie, he put himself between them. They shot him down, then ran."

The woman burst into loud sobs again. Maggie didn't know what to do. She clasped her hands, before finally going over and sitting next to the woman.

The mother cried a moment more on the woman next to her before pulling free and throwing herself into Maggie's arms. Surprised, Maggie stared, then imitated Jake's actions by enfolding the older woman in an embrace. The woman's head slipped down and her hand went to Maggie's stomach as she sobbed. Over the sobbing she heard Jake's voice as he prayed.

Maggie began whispering her own prayers and words of comfort. The people with them were all in various stages of dress. Some wore robes; others were dressed as if they'd been out for a night on the town. They stood around talking, sharing stories, relating over and over what had happened.

At one point Jake went up and spoke to the nurse and then returned. "They're still working on him," he told the group, then comforted those who needed it.

His touch, a gentle word, a look of understanding or just an ear as he listened and soothed, was all that was needed.

When Maggie saw the doctor coming, she knew. It was in his eyes, in the set of his shoulders, in the taut look of his jaw.

Eddie's mama knew, too. She stiffened. "No. Oh, no. No, my Eddie's not dead. *No!*" she wailed.

And then Jake was there along with others, surrounding her. Maggie was jostled until she was near the rear.

Stepping back, she again felt at a loss, until she saw Elaina sitting alone, curled in on herself, silent and still.

Maggie went over to her. She looked about as far along in her pregnancy as Maggie. Maybe a month or two less. Worried, Maggie awkwardly knelt in front of the girl and took her hands. "Are you okay?"

The girl looked up and the pain in her eyes broke Maggie's heart. "He was always telling me one day I was gonna get myself killed hanging around with those no accounts. He told me I didn't know Jesus and I had no business hanging around with people like that 'cause if I died, I wouldn't ever see him again.''

Maggie was stunned to hear that Eddie had shared this with his sister. Eddie, who put on such a tough exterior. Eddie, who was only ten years old. Eddie, sharing the plan of salvation with his family.

"He saved me," the girl whispered. "When that boy came in and was gonna shoot me to get back at my boyfriend, Eddie jumped in front of me. Before he lost consciousness he told me Jesus loved me. Those were his last words."

Maggie reached out and stroked the girl's arms, not sure what to say. *Help me, Father,* she prayed. "He loved you, Elaina," she finally said. "Just like Jesus gave His life for us, your brother was willing to give his for you. So you'd have a chance to open your heart up to God, have a new chance at life."

"I know," the young girl said. "And while I knelt there holding Eddie, I gave my heart to Jesus. But why did he have to die? Why?"

"I don't know. But we are comforted that one day we'll see him again."

The young girl leaned forward, hugged Maggie and began to softly weep. Maggie wept with her.

Maggie wasn't sure how long she knelt there holding Elaina before a friend came over and collected her. She sat back and felt a warm hand touch her shoulder.

Looking up, she saw Jake standing there. His strong hand pulled her up, and he started toward the door. "I offered to stay with them tonight, but they have family members who will. I'll go over tomorrow to discuss the...funeral. They want me to perform the ceremony.''

"How can you do it?'' Maggie whispered as they made the way to the car. "During such a time, holding them, hurting with them...how?''

They approached the car. Maggie turned. Instead of opening the car door, Jake suddenly snagged her; wrapping his arms around her, he held on tight. Maggie realized this wasn't to comfort but for a need of comfort.

Maggie held him, too, stroking his back as silent tears rolled down her face. "Ten years old,'' she murmured.

Jake wept. Deep piercing, the choked sound rose from his chest.

Maggie rocked Jake as she held him and cried with him.

Eventually, he released her and assisted her into the car before climbing in his side. Instead of driving off, he gripped the wheel. Maggie found a tissue and wiped at her eyes.

Jake's voice when it came was so soft she almost didn't hear it at first. "My brother was ten when he died.''

Maggie listened, surprised. He decided to share.

"That's why this center is so important. I want a place for kids like Eddie, kids who don't have anywhere to go and need somewhere to go. Or for kids like Elaina, who, if she'd had somewhere to go, might not have gotten involved with that boy, or for kids like the one from the gang who shot Eddie. A place that's an alternative to the street.''

''She says Eddie's last words were that Jesus loved her.''

Jake shuddered and fresh tears fell.

''She said, she asked Jesus into her heart right there. His death wasn't without reaping results.''

Jake nodded and she had a feeling he was too choked up to talk. Finally he reached out and started the car.

They drove home with the soft music of a gospel tape playing in the background. ''You know, Jake, I'll never forget the look in that mother's eyes. The pain, fear, disbelief.''

Maggie rubbed her stomach. ''No matter how things were, how bad they were, she loved that child.''

''Yes, she did.'' At the intersection, Jake turned back toward home.

''I love my child,'' she finally whispered.

Jake didn't comment.

''I don't think I realized until tonight. But as I watched her, all I could think of was what if that had been my child....''

Maggie rubbed her stomach. ''No matter about...before. *Now* is all that counts. Here and now.''

The church came into sight.

''I'm not giving my baby up, Jake. I know there are things that will have to heal in my heart, but I'm not giving my baby up.''

Jake pulled into her driveway and parked the car.

He came around and helped almost lift her out of the car.

But instead of releasing her, he pulled her until her belly was pressed against him. He wrapped his arms around her and pulled her even closer, then he lowered his head and kissed her.

Maggie felt the rub of his lips as he caressed hers, the comfort, the joy, the celebration of life, even a touch of grief, of loss.

When Jake released her, Maggie was breathless, staring up at him in a daze. "Wow," she whispered.

Jake cupped her cheek. "Yeah, wow."

He leaned forward and kissed her lips again with more tenderness than passion. "I'm happy for you, Maggie. And...thank you...for tonight. For being there for me, and for them."

He pulled her back against him and gave her a long hug, then stepped back. "We should get you to bed. And I don't want you in to work until after noon tomorrow."

"But..."

"No buts, Maggie. You have a baby to think of. I shouldn't have gotten you—"

"I would have been angry if you hadn't."

"Good. Then my decision was right."

He walked her to the stairs and helped her up them. "Let me hear the lock," he said softly.

Maggie turned at the door. "Of course, and good night."

She went in, and the bolt clicked.

With a sigh and a rub of his neck, Jake went back to his car and parked it in his driveway.

After getting out, he slammed the door and started toward his house. Absently he rubbed his fingers together, remembering the touch of her cheek, the softness, the lazy glow in her eyes when she'd looked up in stunned amazement.

Oh, Father, she's the one. I love that woman. And she's going to keep the baby. Jake was happy for her. He couldn't make a decision like that for her. He would have been supportive with whatever decision she made, but the look on her face, the conviction, told him she had settled it in her mind and was certain, so he was happy.

Pausing on the steps, he gazed up at the bright starry sky. "Eddie, not only did you lead your sister to the Lord tonight, but you just gave Maggie a new hope, a new goal. For that, I thank you."

Wearily he went up the stairs, both grief and joy warring in his soul.

Chapter Sixteen

Maggie closed the umbrella as she entered the church. "What a mess," she muttered to Jennifer, who stood there staring out the front windows.

Jennifer nodded. "Isn't it. That storm has been brewing in the Gulf for three days now. It doesn't look like we're going to get any relief from the rain for a while."

"I knew there was a reason I didn't like hurricanes. You'd think this far inland the rain wouldn't reach us." Maggie rubbed at her lower back and sighed.

Jennifer glanced her way. "Back hurting you again?"

Maggie attempted a smile. "It has hurt the entire pregnancy. I think now, though, because I've gotten so big, it hurts constantly."

"Hey, you're only two weeks from delivery. These things happen. Just think, two more weeks and you'll be out of pain and holding that precious child."

Maggie smiled softly and rubbed her stomach. "Yeah. Well, I'd better get to work. I have a ton of typing to catch up on from all those meetings Jake has been attending for the inner-city center."

Jennifer chuckled. "Don't you. He certainly has been busy with that."

"That project means everything to him."

Jennifer nodded. "I know. Gage has worked with him some on it. He's very passionate about it."

Maggie smiled and turned toward her office thinking that much was true. Jake lived and breathed that center. And things were coming together nicely. Maggie was thankful that he understood and didn't force her to attend those meetings.

Two months working with Jake and she had avoided her parents' detection. Maybe they believed she had left the area and weren't going to cause any more problems. After all, she hadn't run into anyone who knew them, nor had she gone anywhere near where they would be.

At one time Maggie thought she'd miss that way of life. She'd felt everything she knew was tied up in that life-style. Now Maggie found this life-style much simpler. She actually enjoyed what she did.

Ruefully she looked down at her fingers. No more manicured nails. They were cut short so she could type fast. She reached up and touched her hair, which she'd pulled back in a ponytail today to keep it out of her face. Gone was the salon cut. Her hair easily hung down to the middle of her back.

Going into the office, she uncovered the computer and unlocked her desk. She slipped off the shirt she'd put over her dress to keep the rain off her, then put the shirt and umbrella on the back of the door handle to the office door.

Maggie checked the plants to make sure they had enough water, brewed some decaffeinated herbal tea, which Jake insisted they drink because of her pregnancy, and then sat down to work.

Two hours later Jake walked in. "Get me the church directory of all our shut-ins. I need to make some calls. Looks like Sheila is turning this way and coming up the mouth of the Mississippi." His words were short, his face creased with worry.

Maggie gaped. "But...but that's almost impossible." She reached in the file and pulled out the church directory, then pushed herself up from her chair.

Jake came back out of the office. "Sit down. You're too far along to be getting up and down."

Maggie scowled. "I'm fine." Halfway up, her lower back twisted and she gasped.

Jake focused his attention on her, going immediately to her side. "Then let me help you up. Maggie-May, you're too stubborn by half. You should take it a little easier."

Maggie lowered herself back into the chair, with Jake's help. Despite what she'd said, it felt good to have his strong hands on her, assisting her. "I've not had any help my entire pregnancy except for your kindness, Jake."

Jake scowled this time. "I only wish I'd been there to help, Maggie-May."

"I didn't mean—"

"I know you didn't," he cut in, his eyes piercing her.

Maggie's mouth went dry. She tried to swallow. Her heart fluttered and her stomach turned. "I— uh—"

"No, Maggie. Don't say anything." He reached out and cupped her cheek. "I told you I wouldn't push and I won't. But it doesn't hurt for you to know I care."

Jake stroked her cheek with his thumb, then stepped back. "Now, that list?"

Belatedly Maggie looked down and realized she had the list, crumbled, in her hands. "Oh."

Jake chuckled. Leaning down, he captured her lips in a soft kiss.

Maggie felt the kiss all the way down to the curling of her toes. *Tenderness.* Oh, how that felt so wonderful. "You shouldn't do that in the office," she whispered.

Jake shook his head. "One day, Maggie, you're gonna learn to trust God and not worry about my reputation for me."

Jake took the list and, with a wink, went into his office.

Maggie watched him shut the door before going back over to flip on the radio for a weather report. It'd been at least seventy or eighty years since a hurricane had come up the river. Possibly longer than that. Maggie had heard stories in history class. But that was it.

As Maggie listened, she typed up the work that had to be done and then printed it up. She found it increasingly hard to get up and down, and wished it wasn't going to go another two weeks because of the way the baby felt.

"A lot of babies go late."

Maggie, who was half standing at her chair and waiting for the muscle cramps in her back to relax, glanced up and saw Elizabeth and Rand at her door. She blushed. "I don't think I'm going to last that much longer. I've discovered muscles I never knew I had."

Elizabeth laughed, the light tinkling sound enriching the office and putting Maggie immediately at ease.

Rand walked toward Jake's door. "Is Jake in? We've come to help with the shut-ins."

Maggie nodded at Rand. "Go on in." She went over to make copies of her reports. "Would you like some tea, Elizabeth?"

Elizabeth took the copies from her and made a shooing motion. "Go sit down and let me finish this. You look tired and don't need to be on your feet."

"Why is everyone treating me like an invalid?" Maggie muttered, waddling back to her desk.

"Because we love you," Elizabeth said. "Are you having trouble sleeping?"

Maggie lowered herself into the chair with relief. "As a matter of fact, I am. It doesn't seem I can ever find a comfortable position."

"You should have carried twins. It was just like that, except that mine were early. The last two months I don't think I slept more than an hour or two at a time. Hiccups, gymnastics, kicks, you name it, the kids were at it.''

Elizabeth brought the papers over to Maggie and then busied herself pouring tea for them. ''Where are the kids?''

''Kaitland is watching them. Max is doing some last-minute things at the office to get it evacuated, and Kaitland knew Rand and I wanted to come help with the shut-ins so she volunteered. Tyler is out there now, making sure the vans are ready to go.''

''Tyler is here?'' Maggie was surprised.

''Yes. We swung by and picked him up on our way.''

''What are you going to do with the shut-ins? Where will you take them?'' Maggie was curious. She couldn't remember her church ever having to do anything like this. Of course, she hadn't worked behind the scenes the way she did here.

''Well, we have families who have volunteered as adoptive families to different people who are unable to get around on their own. Jake is making sure those families are still available. Those who aren't, we'll take them to backup families to stay with. The church has a special widow's fund set up for emergencies. Helping these people during the hurricane will certainly qualify. Some have relatives whom Jake is calling to let know what is going on.''

Maggie nodded. ''They haven't given a mandatory evacuation yet?''

''No. But if the storm keeps coming it'll be here in six hours. It'd be better for us to go ahead and get them out now. If you haven't noticed, the winds out there are already over fifty miles an hour."

"You're kidding." Maggie stared in shock at Elizabeth.

"You haven't been listening to the radio?"

Maggie pushed herself up and came around the desk to make her way toward the front of the church. "Well, yes, but the second line has been ringing off the hook with questions. I had heard twenty-five and thirty miles an hour. But fifty?"

Dark gray clouds hung low in the sky, dropping sheets of rain on the landscape outside. The water was almost horizontal in its direction as the wind blew it off toward the north. "Look at that branch!"

Maggie pointed at a huge tree branch that went flying by.

"Yeah. It's only a matter of time before they order at least a partial evacuation or insist everyone stay inside and off the streets."

Maggie nodded. "I had no idea. The office is very well insulated."

Tyler came running in. "Hello, ladies," he muttered, as he jogged past.

Maggie frowned, worried. She wondered how her parents were and their business. What type of plans were they making? Was everything going to be okay?

Maggie rubbed at her aching sides and then her tummy, wishing at that moment that her parents had accepted her decision. But they hadn't and now wanted nothing to do with her.

"Come on, honey, let's go."

Rand's voice brought Maggie's head around. Tyler,

Rand, Jake and Elizabeth all stood there. It was painful to see the tenderness in Rand's eyes as he gazed down at his wife. Maggie looked over at Jake and saw a knowing look in his eyes.

Maggie glanced back out the door. "You all be careful," she said.

Elizabeth hugged her, and then they were dashing out the door to the vans.

"I hope they're okay."

Jake walked up by her and draped an arm over her shoulders. "I'm sure they will be."

The vans left the parking lot.

"By the way, the Federal Emergency Management Agency just announced a mandatory evacuation. New Orleans is already being flooded with hurricane category four force winds, and the storm hasn't even moved over them yet. They're predicting it'll be here late tonight."

"What about all the people in the hotels here?" Maggie fretted.

Jake sighed. "It looks like they'll be going farther north."

"This is just unbelievable."

"Yeah." Jake steered her back toward the office. "I want you to go home and pack a suitcase. Get everything done you need to do. Consider your day over. I'm going to finish some calls, and then some men are coming to help me board up the windows here and at the houses. I'll be ready to go in two hours at the most. Do you have anyone who can drive you somewhere or do you want to go with me?"

"I'm sure I can find someone...."

Jake shook his head. "I'd rather you go with me. Tyler has a hunting cabin three hours from here. Last time we had a bad hurricane he offered it. A bunch of us from the church met up there. Rand, Elizabeth, Max and Kaitland said they'd be there."

Relieved, Maggie didn't mention that she didn't know anyone in the area and hadn't wanted to call her parents. Besides, if she was honest, she wanted to be with Jake. He made her feel safe. Maggie nodded. "Thank you, Jake."

"No problem. Now, get your umbrella and let's go."

Maggie grabbed the old shirt and umbrella and made her way home. The rain was falling so hard that the umbrella did no good. She was completely soaked by the time she staggered up the stairs.

On the last stair the umbrella became inverted. She grasped at it, fighting it. The wind suddenly gusted and the umbrella went flying right with her. Maggie staggered and went down hard. Panicked, her arms clutched her stomach in protection. Pain streaked through her knees and hip where she'd fallen trying to protect her stomach.

Maggie lay there panting, waiting for the pain to subside before she struggled back up. Sighing heavily, she limped to the door and shoved it open.

"Mmmmrrreeowww."

"Captain Kat! I forgot all about you, sweetie. What are we going to do?"

Maggie shoved the door closed behind her and proceeded to shed her soggy clothes. She was so wet she had to get a towel and dry herself off. The entire time

Captain Kat wove her way in and out of Maggie's feet. "You're worried, too, are you, sweetie? I can't blame you there."

Maggie grabbed her "hospital" suitcase she had packed and carried it to the living room. The baby books Maggie had read told her to have a suitcase ready. It contained two little outfits she'd bought for the baby, plus everything she'd need. She went back into her room and packed a second suitcase. "Hunting cabin? What would they have at a hunting cabin?"

Maggie gathered some sheets and pillowcases. She got some toilet paper and toothpaste and washcloths and detergent. Then she added her own personal items, as well as supplies for Captain Kat.

"Now we wait." Maggie sat down on the couch. She shifted off her tender hip and ignored her stinging knees as she stared out at the bleak gray sky. "Thank you, Father, for the rain, for the beauty it will bring. Protect the people here, Father. Keep harm from them."

The cat came over and, to Maggie's surprise, jumped up in her lap.

Maggie stroked the fur. She ignored the halfhearted growl. "It'll be fine, Captain Kat. Everything is going to be just fine. Jake is going to be here to help us soon."

Kathryn growled. "You know him by name now, do you?" Maggie chuckled. "I think I trust him, Kathryn. I know I trust him," she said, changing her mind. "I just...I can't admit—"

The sound of pounding on her door caused her to jump.

"Come in!"

Jake entered, carrying an extra rain slicker. "This is better than the one you had on that day I met you. It'll cover you to your ankles. Put this on... *aaaachoo.*" Jake eyed the cat balefully. "You can't mean for that cat to..."

"Jake!" Maggie stared, appalled. "I can't leave her here."

Jake sighed, shaking his head in defeat. "Of course not."

"Maybe one of the other families can take her," Maggie offered as she watched Jake sniff.

"No. No, I'll be fine. Let me load everything and then I'll come back for you."

Maggie didn't argue. After her fall she wasn't taking any chances. She rubbed at her aching hip, then her back. Jake, who was in the process of picking up the suitcases, saw her and paused. "Are you okay?"

Guiltily, Maggie looked up. "I slept wrong and my back was aching this morning when I got up. Then on the way over here I, um...fell on the steps."

Jake dropped the suitcases and hurried over. Grabbing her hands, he lifted her arms, looking them over, turning her slightly. "Are you okay? Should we go to the hospital?"

"Jake! I just hurt my hip and pulled the muscles in my back. A warm bath will help. But when we get going, and I'm off my feet, I imagine I'll feel much better."

Jake frowned, then finally nodded. "Okay. Let me

just load the suitcases.'' He went and picked them up, sneezed, then hurried out the house.

Maggie gathered up the cat. She slipped her under the slicker Jake had provided just as he ran back in. His hair was plastered to his head. With a shove he slicked it back, sending water everywhere. ''Come on, Maggie-May.''

Slipping a protective arm around her, he led her out and down the stairs. The cat meowed pitifully. Maggie made soothing noises.

Jake jerked open the door against the harsh gusts and helped her into the car. Kathryn immediately scrambled out and into the back seat in a far corner.

He hurried around the front of the car, fighting the wind as he climbed in. Jake started the car and then paused, his eyes on the church.

Maggie watched different emotions flit through his eyes. ''The church is in our hearts, Jake. Even if the building isn't around when we get back, the church will still be here.''

Jake nodded, turned the car and started down the road, away from their home and toward the shelter.

Maggie said a soft prayer that everything would work out according to God's will.

Chapter Seventeen

"This is the third detour we've had to make," Jake grumbled.

Maggie didn't mean to sound panicked, but she was beginning to worry. "Maybe we should have turned left back at that last highway." Maggie shifted uncomfortably and looked at the harsh rain sweeping across the small country road.

"No, this is the right way."

Maggie hoped he was right. As far as she could tell, they were in the middle of nowhere. Of course, most cabins were in the middle of nowhere, so maybe he was correct. She shifted again.

Jake noticed. "Are you okay?"

"My back is hurting from sitting in the car so long, I'm afraid. And well—" Maggie blushed "—I have to, um, go to the bathroom."

"I'm sorry, Maggie. I didn't think. We've been on the road for hours and you being pregnant and all..."

Jake flushed. "We'll be at the cabin in twenty minutes or less. However, I'll watch for something along—"

The swaying trees chose that moment to object to their mistreatment by the weather.

"Jake, watch out!" Maggie grabbed the dash, bracing herself, and watched in slow motion as one huge branch fell right into their path.

Jake jerked his head back around. He slammed on the brakes.

The car skidded and then crashed over the branch. Maggie gasped as she was tossed up and down, then sideways.

The car came to an abrupt halt and was silent.

"Are you all right?"

Dazed, Maggie looked over at Jake, who was yanking on his seat belt. He got it released and reached for her. Maggie shakily released her own seat belt and went into his arms.

"Oh, Maggie-May, I'm so sorry."

"It's not your fault," she murmured into his chest. His warmth invaded her, surrounded her, reassured her. "I guess we shouldn't be surprised after all the downed branches we've passed on the way. No one ever expects trouble to happen to them, though."

Jake suddenly sneezed.

"Mrreeeooowww."

"Oh!" Maggie pulled back. Captain Kat sat on the seat next to Jake's shoulder, licking her paw. At Maggie's attention, she paused and meowed again. Maggie smiled, relieved. "The cat came through it fine."

Jake nodded. "I see that." He glanced nervously at the cat.

The cat saw his look and growled.

Jake shuddered at the sound, then turned his attention from the cat. "It appears we didn't come through it fine."

Maggie finally noticed the way the car leaned. Glancing around, she saw that the rear of the vehicle was partially in a ditch. "Oh, no, can we get out?"

"I don't know. Stay here while I check it out." Jake grabbed his raincoat from the back seat and hopped out, then slipped the coat on. She watched him go to the back and then he disappeared from view.

Absently, Maggie accepted Captain Kat's need for love and reassurance when she crawled into Maggie's lap, and Maggie stroked her. "He'll be fine. I'm sure the car is okay."

Jake stood and moved around the car. He stopped at the front and disappeared from sight again. When he stood back up, there was a scowl on his face.

Maggie shifted uncomfortably, not wanting to hear bad news. "It seems I may not get to a bathroom in the next fifteen or twenty minutes, Kathryn, if the expression on Jake's face is any indication."

The cat growled.

"Stop that, Kathryn. That's not nice."

Obviously offended by Maggie's reprimand, the cat wiggled loose and returned to the back window seat.

Just in time, too. Jake pulled open the door and slipped in.

"What's the matter?"

Jake shoved at his hair, wiping a hand down his face. "It looks like we won't be going anywhere, Maggie. The axle is broken."

Maggie stared at Jake in shock. "You're kidding."

Wearily, Jake looked at her. "I only wish I were."

Maggie suddenly giggled.

"What do you find so amazing about that statement?"

Maggie shook her head. "It's not the statement, exactly, that made me laugh."

"Oh? Then what?"

Maggie's cheeks heated. "It's that, well, despite the fact that we are stranded here and a hurricane is on the way, the only thing I can think of is that I have to go to the bathroom."

Jake stared for a moment, before his features relaxed and he chuckled. "Only you, Maggie-May. Only you."

Maggie's chuckle turned into a snort. "Only any pregnant woman who has a seven-pound baby or so sitting on her bladder. So, what are we going to do?"

Jake smiled and reached across Maggie into the glove compartment. "Cell phone."

"Oh, thank goodness," Maggie said. "I might just find a bathroom."

Jake chuckled and flipped the cell on. He listened—and frowned.

"Then again—" Jake flipped it on and off several times. "I'm afraid, Maggie, you're going to have to wait a little longer."

Maggie smothered a laugh of disbelief. "Now what?"

Jake shrugged. "Stay here and hope someone comes by?"

Maggie shifted, arching her back and trying to get comfortable. "I suppose that's one option...."

"Well, we have prayer, too."

Maggie agreed and said a quick prayer for help. Despite her words to Jake, she could not sit in this car until someone came. Her back was killing her. Her bladder was killing her. Her whole body was stiff from the fall. She had to get out, and soon, or she was going to go crazy.

Jake suddenly leaned forward, peering out the windshield into the distance. "Look, there, that looks like a possible road...."

Maggie followed where Jake pointed to a dirt track. "More like a hewn path to me."

"Exactly, which means it's not a traveled road but probably a driveway."

Just then Maggie spotted it. "Over there, almost back behind us. It curves around."

"Answered prayers," Jake murmured. Turning, he asked Maggie, "Can you make it there?"

Maggie gave Jake a long-suffering look. "I'm pregnant not—"

"Helpless. Yes, I know. You keep telling me that."

"Then let's go." Maggie picked up the cat.

Jake grimaced, then sneezed.

"You know, I think you're right. I don't think you're allergic to cats."

"I'm not."

Maggie smiled. "It's a psychological thing."

"It is not." Jake looked at her aghast. "The cat

just needs a bath. It probably picked up some pollen or something.''

''Uh-huh. Of course, Jake.''

''If we're going to take it, let me carry her. You shouldn't be walking that far carrying her.'' Jake had a stubborn little boy look, as if he were set to prove something.

Maggie rolled her eyes. ''I can do it.''

Jake shook his head determinedly. ''I'll do it.''

Maggie was certain this was tied up in some macho thing, so she let him. ''Fine. Here you go.'' She held out Kathryn.

''The cat is growling—again.''

Maggie shrugged, smiling sweetly. ''She doesn't bite—I don't think.''

''You don't think?''

''She has never bitten me.''

''Great.'' Jake took the cat, the hair on his neck shooting up.

The cat growled louder, her voice going up and down the range of sounds.

''You know, Jake, I really can carry her. You don't have to.''

Jake shook his head. ''We're fine. Aren't we, Captain Kat?''

Maggie reached in the back seat, grabbed her raincoat and awkwardly slipped it on, which wasn't any easier than having divested herself of it earlier. Finally she had it on. Glancing at the still-growling cat and the sneezing Jake, who looked as though he was afraid he was going to die any moment, she sighed. ''I'm ready.''

Jake nodded, hesitated, then shoved the cat into his raincoat. Pushing his door open, he said, "Stay right there. I'll be around."

Maggie didn't argue. She shoved open her own door and wiggled to the edge of the seat, then slowly hauled herself out of the car. When she stood, she gasped and grabbed at her back.

"I told you to wait! Are you okay?" Jake, face creased in concern, reached out for her.

Maggie willingly leaned into him. "My back is killing me. I guess when I fell I really pulled some muscles."

Jake slipped an arm around her. "Come on, let's get up there. We'll get permission to sit out the storm with these people, and then I'll come back for our suitcases."

Maggie nodded. For some reason, walking was much slower. Water soaked her feet and legs, and the baby was so low that every step seemed to take twice as long. On the driveway they had to battle the mud. "This is really disgusting. Mud is oozing in my shoes."

"You think you've got problems. I've got four sets of claws permanently embedded in my chest."

"Oh, Jake!"

"And she's still growling. How you didn't keep from having a nervous breakdown before now I'll never understand. She's making me a nervous wreck."

Maggie chuckled despite the pain in her back. "All bark and no bite, Jake."

"She's not barking, Maggie."

Maggie squeezed Jake's side reassuringly. "Just stop worrying. I offered to carry her."

They arrived at the door and knocked. Maggie stepped away and tried to shake the water from her coat. "My stomach's wet."

Maggie looked in disgust where the coat hadn't covered her bulging stomach.

Jake sneezed, pulled Kathryn out of his own coat and handed the cat to her. "Hold her while I knock."

Maggie smiled. "Have you ever heard the saying 'Like me, like my cat'?"

Jake knocked on the door, glancing at Maggie in surprise. "Actually, the way I heard the saying went was—"

"You don't have to like my cat, Jake, to like me," Maggie hurriedly interrupted. "Not everyone is a cat lover." Maggie leaned against the wall, bending one leg as her back cramped.

"I don't think anyone is at home."

Dismayed, Maggie stared at Jake. "You're kidding."

Jake shook his head. He knocked again and waited. "I hear nothing from inside, and there are no cars around."

The pain in Maggie's back abated, but her leg was cramping from standing so oddly so she walked across the porch to ease the cramp from her thigh. "I can't wait. If they're not home I'm going to have to find a tree."

Jake chuckled. "Take your pick."

Maggie looked around at the many, many trees. "It's raining," she said in disgust.

"There's a hurricane coming, Maggie."

She heard the laughter in his voice. "Oh, is there, Jake? I thought we were just driving along for the fun of it." Maggie shook her head and shoved the cat at Jake.

Captain Kat meowed in objection.

Jake sneezed.

Maggie smiled. "I'll be right back." Maggie shifted and rubbed at her back before going to the edge of the porch. She peered out, then carefully made her way down the stairs. "Oh, ugh... Oh!"

Maggie froze.

Jake, who was still trying to adjust the cat and keep her claws out of his flesh, looked up.

Maggie met his eyes.

"What is it, Maggie-May?"

Dismayed, Maggie moved her raincoat to check her legs. Jake followed her gaze.

"I guess you really weren't kidding about having to go to the bathroom."

Maggie lifted her gaze to Jake. "I still have to go to the bathroom."

Jake stared, then motioned to her pants, which were soaking wet.

Maggie shook her head. "I *still* have to go to the bathroom.

Maggie watched as Jake's eyes suddenly widened and his gaze riveted on her legs once more.

"Oh, no. Don't you dare tell me that, Maggie..."

He was begging. Maggie had to smile. She had never heard that note in a man's voice before. It was edged with panic, the same panic she was feeling.

Father, we don't need two of us panicking, she whispered. Taking a deep breath, she nodded at Jake, whose gaze was now locked to hers. "I'm sorry, Jake. My water just broke."

Jake shook his head.

Maggie nodded. "I'm afraid so. It looks like I'm going to have my baby."

Chapter Eighteen

Jake broke out a window.

"What are you doing?"

Jake didn't care that Maggie stared at him so oddly. He was worried sick. A baby. He couldn't believe it. "You cannot have your baby right now. I'll pay these people back. But we're getting in and calling for help."

Jake pushed the window open and crawled through. In seconds he was pulling open the door.

Jake took one look at Maggie standing there and reached out to guide her in. This could not be happening.

Jake ran a hand over his face. "Just sit down or something and I'll be right back." Glancing at her stomach, he thought she still seemed just like everyday Maggie. And yet her water had broken, and she was telling him she was going to have a baby. He gulped and turned toward the kitchen.

He was grateful when he found a phone in there. *Oh, Father, please don't let her have this child now. Why? Why is this happening?* Things couldn't get any worse. *I don't understand, Father.*

Jake picked up the phone.

There was no dial tone.

Jake stared at the phone in disbelief. "God!" He actually looked up at the ceiling. "What is going on here?"

All he saw was plaster, though he knew God had heard him.

Trust me. A sweet soft voice floated to him from within. With that voice a gentle peace surrounded Jake.

"Father, Father, Father, I don't know what to do. This is just beyond belief. Please, Father, help me here."

Jake shook his head. "Tyler's cabin—it's only an hour away, maybe more...."

But Jake knew he wasn't going to take a pregnant woman in labor out into this mess.

Why? he whispered.

Jake fought and slowly forced himself to accept the situation. Then he turned and went in to tell Maggie...and found her just coming out of the bathroom.

"Maggie! What are you doing? You are about to have a baby!"

Maggie jumped and grabbed at her heart. "Don't yell like that, Jake!"

She stared at him and he felt his cheeks heat up. He couldn't believe he'd raised his voice. Wearily he ran a hand over his face, thinking panic was doing neither one of them any good.

It didn't help when Maggie laughed at him. "Jake, it's my first child. They say those labors take up to fourteen or fifteen hours—" Maggie suddenly gasped and grabbed her stomach, her eyes widening.

Jake almost swallowed his tongue. So much for staying calm. Seeing Maggie's face contort as she grabbed her stomach like that gave him palpitations. "What is it?"

Maggie glanced ed up. "That one was much stronger than the others."

Jake felt sweat break out on his forehead, even though cool wind blew in through the window. Then her words registered. "Others?" His voice sounded odd even to his own ears.

Maggie smiled sheepishly. He wanted to tell her not to look at him like that. That look meant trouble. No, he didn't like that look at all and braced himself for whatever she was getting ready to say.

She didn't disappoint him, either.

"I didn't know before, but now I think the pain in my back these last nine or ten hours must have been contractions. It only got worse when the water broke. I mean, it's coming all the way around—"

Maggie gasped again, her eyes widening.

"Don't do that!" Jake reached out, paused, then reached out again for her. Watching her, his stomach lurched. He didn't like the thought that she was in pain at all.

"Do what?" she said, panting.

"Widen your eyes as though you're about to drop

that baby any minute.'' He also didn't like that he was the only person in the area and that Maggie was in labor. It hit him blindingly at that moment—the reason he didn't like it: he was so in love with this woman that he couldn't bear the thought of losing her.

Please, Father, guide me. He'd never in his life delivered a baby and here was his Maggie, about to deliver her child.

Maggie looked incredulous, drawing Jake's attention back to her. "I'm not about to *drop* this baby. Fourteen hours or so of labor, Jake. Remember?''

"You just said you'd been in labor a good ten hours,'' Jake reminded her. He watched Maggie as his words dawned on her.

"Oh, my,'' she whispered.

Jake's hope that they might get out of this without anything happening sank to his toes. But as his hope sank, a strange peace descended, too. Jake suddenly felt in control and able to cope. Maggie had no one else. God never put more on them than they could bear. God would see them through this. Jake smiled, moved forward and slipped a gentle arm around Maggie.

"So, when will the ambulance be here?'' she asked, leaning her small frame against him. Jake held her, enjoying the feel of this woman depending on him.

Jake swallowed. Maggie sounded so hopeful and the cat, sitting there by her, looked expectant, too. Reluctantly, he turned Maggie toward the couch and helped her down to a sitting position.

"Well?'' she asked, gazing up at him expectantly.

Gently he broke the news. "The phones aren't working."

"Don't tell me that!"

Mirrored in her eyes was the panic he'd felt only moments before. He wanted to pull her back up into his arms and hold her, tell her everything was okay. Instead he said jokingly, "The phones were taken when the people left."

"You're kidding!" Maggie glanced up, incredulous.

He watched her slowly relax as the contraction left. "Yes, I am, Maggie-May. You told me not to tell you the phones weren't working."

Dumbfounded, she stared. "You're telling me a joke at a time like this?"

Jake smiled. "Seemed the best thing to do."

Maggie fell back against the couch and laughed. "Oh, Jake. What am I going to do with you? A joke!" Wearily she shook her head.

Jake sat down next to her and took her hand. It looked so small in his larger one; it was soft and gentle. He rubbed his thumb over the top of it, noting how pale her skin was next to his darker tone. He heard her breath catch and slowly lifted his steady gaze to her fearful one. "We'll make it though this, Maggie-May. I'll go out and see if I can locate another cabin nearby and contact the authorities for help. I'll also get your suitcase so you can change."

Maggie held on to his hand, gripping it. Jake wondered if she knew how much that mirrored the fear in her eyes that she tried to hide behind a weak smile.

"Thank you. I'm sorry about this, Jake. I guess the baby and God have their own time."

Jake leaned forward and placed a gentle kiss on her forehead. "I'll be right back." He stood and grabbed his raincoat. Slipping into it, he went to the door, cast one last look at her, then left.

Maggie watched him leave. When the door was closed she leaned back against the couch with her hands cradling her abdomen. So many emotions swirled through her mind. It was one thing to say she wanted to keep the baby but another to face what had happened to precipitate in the actual birth of that child.

Maggie hugged her stomach, fighting the fears of what-if....

Everything would work out fine. She had to believe that. She had to concentrate on that right now. Jake would find someone and call and they'd have help and everything would be okay.

Maggie went into the bathroom and washed her face, then braided the mass of curls to keep it out of the way while she waited for Jake to return.

When he wasn't back by the time she'd finished with her hair, she waddled into the kitchen and rummaged through the cabinets, taking stock. She was uneasy going through someone else's cabinets. But anything to keep her mind occupied was better than sitting in the living room worrying.

It was twenty-two minutes and eight contractions later before Jake returned. And of course he would walk in when she was bent over, making an awful face.

"Maggie!" Jake dropped the suitcases and rushed over to her.

Maggie, who'd had enough time to calm down, raised a hand, concentrating on her breathing.

Jake stopped and waited.

When the contraction eased she stood. One glance at him told her no help was forthcoming. "No one?" she asked, unable to believe the frustration and defeat etched deeply on his face.

"Not a soul."

Jake retrieved the suitcases, moved to the first bedroom and set them alongside the wall. He took his and went to another bedroom. "Not that I'm planning on being here that long, but you never know. Not one car passed while I was out there."

Jake returned to the living room and set up the cat's food and water.

Captain Kat walked over, sniffed the bowl, turned her tail up and walked off.

Jake plopped his hands on his hips. "I'm the one allergic, and she acts as though I've offended her!"

Maggie chuckled, dryly. "Don't worry. She'll be fine."

His exasperation faded. "Maggie—"

"I know. What are we going to do?"

"Do you trust me?"

Maggie's heart clenched. *Do you trust me?* How long had it been since she'd trusted a man? Oh, she trusted Jake, to a point. But this condition, the problem, made her so vulnerable. "I, we don't have a choice."

Jake smiled, though there was concern in his eyes. "We'll have to help each other. I've, um, well…"

Maggie's attention was caught with the way he walked over to the window and started fiddling to close and cover it.

"I've been reading up on pregnancy and childbirth. The Lamaze method sounds easy enough, as does the delivery."

Maggie couldn't help but stare at his back in shock. "And when did you start reading up on this?" she had to ask.

"A few months ago. With so many women pregnant at the church all the time, I found it an interesting subject."

Maggie's heart softened and melted. She walked forward and touched Jake's shoulder. "You may have just saved this child's life with that knowledge, Jake. Thank you…"

Her hand tightened on his shoulder, and she broke off as another contraction hit her.

Jake turned and cradled her until the contraction had passed. "Your suitcase is in the bedroom. Do you want to change? By the way, I left a note in the car where we were. So, if someone stops by, they'll come here, hopefully."

Maggie nodded. "I'd love to change. I'll be right back."

Maggie went into the room and opened her suitcase. Digging through it, she found a loose housedress and slipped into it. She debated underwear. "This is so embarrassing," she whispered.

Thinking about Jake delivering her baby, she

wanted to groan with mortification. Of course, help still might come. Somehow, though, Maggie knew Jake was going to have to deliver this baby.

Another contraction hit just as she was turning back to the door. Sinking down onto the side of the bed, she groaned.

Jake tapped on the door. "Maggie?"

Maggie's face scrunched up with pain. Dimly she heard the door open, but the contraction consumed her. She felt supportive hands on her shoulders.

"Breathe," the voice whispered.

Realizing she held her breath, Maggie concentrated on breathing. This contraction was worse than the others, she thought vaguely. When it faded she sat back, grateful. "That one..." Maggie shook her head. "I can't imagine them getting worse." She looked up at Jake for reassurance.

He hesitated, then reached for her hand. "Let's walk through the cabin, or maybe go out on the front porch."

Maggie nodded, thinking it a wonderful idea.

"Just how far apart are the contractions?"

"About three minutes." Maggie moved slowly to the door.

Jake opened it.

"I know they weren't this close before my water broke," she confided.

Jake frowned. "Perhaps the labor has increased, or they were that close but you just didn't notice them because they weren't as painful?"

Maggie went out on the porch and over to the railing. Rain fell in a downpour. "Sounds like someone crunching up a paper bag, doesn't it?'' she said softly, soaking in the beauty of the rain.

"I don't know. To me, it sounds like a brook or a dripping faucet.''

Maggie looked over to where Jake pointed and saw a large stream of water flowing. "Isn't it amazing how many sounds there are that God created?''

Another contraction hit. Maggie's hands tightened on the railing. Jake moved up and rubbed a hand up and down her back.

"Oh, that...feels...good.''

Jake's hand moved back down to her lower back. "Here?''

Maggie nodded. "Yes.''

The contraction subsided. Maggie relaxed and sighed. "It was raining that night...''

Jake slipped an arm around her but, she moved away. "What, Maggie?''

Maggie stared out into the rain. Her jaw tensed. She looked so alone, so lost.

"I didn't think I could ever stand the sound of rain again. But having you here with me—it makes things different.''

When her hands tightened on the railing, Jake carefully moved forward and rubbed her back, offering silent support.

Maggie closed her eyes. "I'm so scared, Jake. What if... Can a child conceived in violence... Can I really love the child?''

Jake's jaw tightened and rage ran through him as his fears were confirmed. "Oh, Maggie....''

The contraction faded and she turned into his arms,

faster than he would have thought possible for a woman in labor. He didn't mind. He needed to hold her as much as she needed to be held.

They stood like that through several contractions, Jake holding her, trying to help ease both her physical and emotional pain as her contractions got closer together and her sobs continued.

Finally, Jake began to sing softly, a song of God's love as they stood there. Minute by minute, Maggie's tears quieted and Jake's anger faded.

"Please don't hate me," Maggie murmured when she could talk again.

Jake shook, unable to believe the soft words that mixed with the tumultuous sounds of the storm around them. "Hate you? Hate you! Maggie, how could I hate you for what someone did to you?"

Maggie opened her mouth to reply. A gasp escaped, instead. Here eyes widened and she looked to Jake, sudden dismay and fear in her eyes. "Oh...oh! This...is...not the time...to tell...you this."

Jake forced his anger at the unknown assailant aside, trying to hold Maggie as she sobbed and help her through another contraction. "Come on, sweetheart, let's get you inside."

Maggie groaned. "Oh, Jake...something is different."

Jake's anger fled completely, replaced by fear. "What? What is it?"

Maggie grabbed at her lower stomach. "I'm not sure. But I think, it may be time, to have the baby."

Chapter Nineteen

Jake helped Maggie into the cabin and then to the bedroom. "Lie down, Maggie."

Maggie turned and slowly lowered herself to the bed. Then she grabbed Jake's arms as another contraction hit. "Ooooh..."

"Breathe," he said gently, putting action with words and breathing with her. When the contraction subsided, he said very matter-of-factly, "Maggie, hon, I need to check you."

Maggie's face went up in flames. "This is so awful," she said mournfully. "What is your congregation going to think?"

Jake laughed. "You're worried about what my congregation is going to think at a time like this?"

Maggie's embarrassment left and she scowled. "Stop laughing."

Jake liked her anger better than her embarrassment.

Pushing her legs up, he moved her dress enough to carefully check her. "I see something…"

Maggie gasped. "Con-trac-tion!"

Jake reached out and grasped her flailing hand. "They won't disapprove, dear."

"I…really…hate that word…*dear*," she gasped. "*He* used to always call me that." She surged up, grabbing at Jake's arms. "Oh, dear—oh dear—oh, dear, this hurts!"

"Breathe like this," he said, and took slow deep breaths, staring at her, willing her to imitate his actions.

"He said that to me the night after he was done. 'We're going to be married, dear. What are you so upset about?' My parents said it to me when I told them what had happened. 'Rape, dear? You just don't want to pay the piper now that you've gotten caught.'"

Maggie fell back, gasping anew. "They have ruined every job I've tried to get, making sure I got fired. If they had found out I was your secretary, they would have made sure you fired me, too, with the explanation 'Sorry, dear, but you should really leave the area until your little matter is taken care of.'"

Jake stroked her head, vowing to throttle her parents if he ever met them. He was outraged, warring with his own feelings as he listened. The only thing that kept him from voicing his anger was his years of counseling. Maggie didn't need his anger as much as she needed to pour out her own anger and fears.

"I hate him, Jake. I hate him. My parents hurt me, but I hate him."

Maggie cried. Jake stroked her forehead, her cheeks, her hair. "Shh, Maggie-May. It's over. Let God heal you."

"I know what people think about me. I'm pregnant, single and deserved this."

"No, Maggie. Never. No one ever deserved that."

"I was taking him home from a party. He wanted to go into my house for a minute. My parents were always having him over for dinner since he's an associate. I let him kiss me...."

Jake cupped her face, then held her as she went through another contraction. While she was trying to breathe, he said, "Maggie, I don't care if you were standing before him naked. If you said no, then no is no. I don't care if you were both in bed together, no is still no. I don't care if he had been your husband. *No is still no.*"

Maggie, her gaze filled with hurt, locked eyes with him. "It was on the couch, in the den. He hurt me, Jake, and didn't care. No one cared. He kept telling me I had led him on." Maggie shuddered. "I was so helpless. He held me down. And though I had thought I was in control of my life, I realized then I had no control. I couldn't get him off me."

Jake pulled Maggie into his arms and held her while she cried. She went through two more contractions as she cried. He silently cried along with her.

"My parents have controlled my life since then, getting me fired. I'm bad luck, dangerous to anyone around me."

"No, Maggie. Don't say that."

Maggie shook her head, her face twisting as another contraction hit. Jake was certain she was in transition.

"What will I do if, when I see this child, I can't love it?"

"Take it one day one minute at a time, Maggie."

Maggie nodded, then gasped falling back. "Jake. I have *got* to push!"

Jake swallowed. "Just a minute." He checked her once more. "Give me two minutes. Breathe through the next contraction and then I'll check you again."

He checked her again and sure enough she was definitely crowning. He jumped up and raced to the bathroom to grab some towels, then went to the kitchen and found a knife.

"Jake!"

The urgency in her voice caused Jake to sprint back into the room. Maggie was trying to breathe through another contraction. Tension etched lines on her damp face, which was covered with a fine sheen of perspiration. He thought she was beautiful at this moment. "We're ready, Maggie-May."

Maggie cried out and grabbed at her knees. "Please save my baby, Jake. Don't let it die."

"God will protect it, Maggie-May," Jake whispered, and began to pray.

Checking her again, he saw a good portion of head crowning. "This is it, sweetheart. Here it comes."

"You don't, have to tell—*me*—that!" Maggie groaned and pushed.

Jake reached down and placed his hand on the top of the infant's head to steady it. Slowly the head emerged. A tiny scrunched-up face with dark hair slicked down against the scalp slipped out into his hand. The nose was so small, and the little eyes were closed. "Oh, Maggie, darlin', it's beautiful. Push again. Let's get the shoulders…that's it…"

First one shoulder then the other came out. And finally the child just slipped into his hands. Jake took a piece of sheet and wiped at the baby's mouth. Amazingly enough, the child let out a loud squall. "Maggie, darlin', you have a girl. And she is the prettiest little girl I've ever seen…next to you."

Maggie looked up, and Jake held the baby where she could see it.

Joy lit up her face, and despite being covered with sweat and obviously exhausted, she laughed. "Oh, she's beautiful."

Maggie reached for her.

"Just let me cut the cord here." Jake tied the small pieces of sheet tightly in two spots and then used the butcher knife to slice the cord. Oddly enough, it was cutting that cord that made him nauseous. He felt faint as he severed the life supply of the child from the mother.

After wrapping the baby in a towel, he handed her up to Maggie.

"Thank you, Father," she whispered.

Jake thought she'd just answered her earlier question. Despite the circumstances of the conception, Maggie's heart had healed, and she was able to love this child.

"What are you going to name her?"

Turning back to the duty at hand, he delivered the rest of the afterbirth and wrapped it in a towel.

"Alyssa."

Jake paused in his actions to smile softly at Maggie. "That's a beautiful name, Maggie, honey."

Maggie smiled tiredly as she touched the baby's cheek. Moving up next to her, Jake wiped her face and neck with a fresh cloth before taking the baby and cleaning her up.

Maggie laughed when the baby cried. "She doesn't like that."

Jake shook his head. "No, she doesn't."

He wrapped the baby in a fresh towel.

"I have some diapers in the suitcase, as well as clothing and towels and sheets. Oh, Jake, why didn't I think of all of this before?"

"Like me, you were expecting to be rescued."

He went to the suitcase and rummaged around until he found what they required, then returned to her side. After taking the infant awkwardly, he laid her back down on the bed between them. "You know, I've handled this baby more than I've handled any other infant."

Maggie chuckled. "I wouldn't know. You handle her like a professional."

Jake put the plastic diaper on and then slipped the generic white gown with yellow bunnies onto Alyssa. The entire time Alyssa squalled. When he wrapped her back in the blanket, she quieted. He slipped her back next to Maggie.

Maggie blinked sleepily. "Thank you, Jake."

Jake smiled and touched her cheek. "My pleasure."

Maggie's eyes drifted closed.

Jake watched her for a long time and then got up and moved to leave the room. Her next words, though, caused him to freeze in place.

"I love you, you know."

They were barely murmured, but when he turned around, Maggie was looking at him.

He nodded. "And I love you."

He didn't break eye contact until her eyes shut. When she was breathing softly, he left the room.

She loved him. Jake's heart sang. *Thank you, Father, for that gift. For* both *gifts.*

In the other room he found a drawer and collected an extra pillow. He made a bed in the drawer for the baby, covered it with one of Maggie's sheets and quietly lifted the baby from her mother.

After taking Alyssa back into the other room, he slipped her into the drawer on her back. He reached out and felt the child to make sure she wasn't too cold, then sat on the couch next to the drawer, watching the baby while Maggie rested.

"Mmmrrreow."

Jake glanced over and saw the cat, near her food dish, staring at him. "Don't give me a look like it's my job to feed you and you're insulted that your food dish is empty. You positively stuck your nose in the air earlier when I filled the dish."

"Mmmrreeoooooow."

Jake sighed. He was not going to pay any attention to that cat, which had snubbed him and tried to scare the stuffing out of him from day one. No way, no how—

"Mmmmeeeeooooooow."

Except that Maggie would want the cat fed.

He stood up and walked past the cat, scowling. "Fine. Fine. But I only fed you an hour ago." Actually, Jake was glad the cat was no longer growling at him. And he was just a tad happy that she actually ate the food. Maybe he and this cat could get along after all.

Jake picked up the container of food and returned to fill the bowl. "There you go."

The cat sniffed, turned around and twitched her tail before walking off.

Jake gaped. "Stubborn cat," he muttered, then promptly sneezed.

The cat crossed the room and hopped up next to the baby.

Jake's heart tripped. He felt ill at ease that this cat was near the baby. He strode across the room, intending to shoo the cat away. But it proved unnecessary. The cat sniffed the baby, nudged her with her nose, then walked off.

Relieved, Jake sat down again next to the baby. "So, little one, I had wondered what your mommy is going to name you. I think Alyssa is a fine strong name."

The baby snuffled her face against the pillow and let out a tiny breath.

Jake melted, watching her. Reaching out, he stroked the dark cap of hair with one finger. His hand was nearly as big as the baby's head. Awed, he stroked the soft skin of her rounded little cheek and then touched the tiny hand. Five perfectly formed little fingers curled around the offering and held on.

"You're going to be a heartbreaker, sweetheart. I can already tell that."

The baby shuddered again softly, making little grunting noises.

Jake chuckled.

A sudden *thunk* outside caught his attention. He stood and moved over to the window. Looking out, he noted it was already darkening and the rain was still pouring. In a few hours the brunt of the hurricane would be there. His guess would be four or five in the morning.

Jake wondered how his little church had survived and how the people of the community who had refused to leave had fared. Worse hit was down closer to New Orleans and such.

A tree branch cracked somewhere in the distance.

A crash outside indicated a tree off in the forest had fallen. Jake stood for what surely was an hour, just communing with his heavenly Father, thanking Him, talking to Him, discussing trivial things with Him.

Finally, Jake turned his back on the storm outside, peace within him, guiding him to trust and depend on God. Realizing the electricity would certainly go out, he found lanterns and brought them into the room; they would probably need them later.

The cat followed him with her eyes, watching his every move from atop the chest in the living room.

Jake continued to sneeze occasionally but found his allergies didn't seem as bad as when he'd first met the cat. "Maybe it was psychosomatic, Captain Kat. You do have a way of doing your best to put people off. Personally," he continued as he finished up with the lanterns, "I think you were somehow behind it. You probably emitted some allergy type scent, didn't you?"

"Jake," Maggie said.

He heard the soft call and then the chuckle that followed and turned. Maggie stood, looking rumpled and exhausted, leaning against the door frame. The overhead light gave her an ethereal look. She glowed from where she stood.

"What are you doing out of bed?" Jake hurried over and slipped an arm around her.

"I've got to have a shower and change."

Jake stared in disbelief. "Surely you aren't strong enough."

Maggie willingly leaned against Jake. "If you'll stand just outside the door, I'll let you know. Would you do that for me?"

Jake debated scooping her up and putting her right back in bed, then shook his head. He was being over-protective. Of course she wanted a bath. The work he'd witnessed her put to bring forth that baby was more work than he put in during an entire month. "Okay, Maggie-May. Go on and I'll be right here if you need me."

Maggie paused, looking at Alyssa. "How is she? I noticed you had taken her out of the room when I fell asleep."

Jake felt a slight flush. "I wanted you to get some rest."

Maggie nodded.

"She's fine. Hasn't woken up yet, though she has been grunting a bit more the past few minutes."

Maggie smiled. "Good."

Jake's heart squeezed at the love in Maggie's eyes. "You'd better go ahead and get that bath before she gets hungry."

Maggie's cheeks turned pink. "I had thought about nursing her if I kept her. It looks like I have no choice now."

Maggie walked slowly back into her room and dug through her suitcase. Jake stayed back and allowed her some privacy. Then she went into the bathroom.

He heard the water run. In minutes the water was cut and he heard her moving around. "Are you okay?"

Her muffled reply reached his ears and then the door was pulled open. Dressed in a soft yellow gown with tiny rosebuds of various colors, she stood there, looking utterly exhausted but absolutely beautiful.

"You've had enough," he said, and scooped her up in his arms.

"Jake," Maggie protested.

"You just rest and let me play knight in shining armor."

Maggie subsided, laying her head down against Jake's shoulder and wrapping her arms around his neck.

"You are tired, aren't you, Maggie-May?"

Maggie nodded against his shoulder. "Some."

Jake went over to the couch and eased her down onto it. After releasing her, he grabbed a pillow and helped her adjust it behind her head, then whipped out a sheet and covered her.

"I can do this myself, Jake—"

Jake smiled and cupped her cheek. "Humor me."

Maggie nodded again. Glancing toward the window, she asked, "How's the weather?"

Jake accepted the change in topic. "Getting bad. I imagine we've got two or three more hours before the brunt of the storm hits."

A small scuffling sound and then a tiny whimper drew their attention to the tiny infant in the drawer.

Maggie pushed up and reached over to retrieve the baby. Awkwardly she held her before pulling it up against her. She jiggled Alyssa a bit to quiet her down.

Instead, the baby squirmed and the whimpering turned to small protests.

Maggie looked up at Jake. "She's not quieting down. What do you suppose is the matter?"

"Maybe her diaper?" Jake went into the other room and got one of the diapers she had brought. He grabbed the wipes and reentered the room. "Here we go. Want me to change her for you?"

Maggie shrugged. "Do you know how?"

Jake studied Maggie and realized she was nervous. It dawned on him that Maggie had never been around children. "I've seen a few changed. It's really easy. Swing your feet around here and help me."

Jake moved the drawer to the table by the couch and then sat down.

Maggie moved her feet and sat up.

After taking the baby, Jake laid the fussy child between them. "Don't worry about the cries. All babies cry."

Jake wasn't an expert, but he wanted to reassure Maggie and put her at ease. And he did know babies cried.

He cleaned the infant, finding this a totally different experience from all the other children he'd had a chance to tend to in his lifetime.

When he was done, he handed the baby back to Maggie and went and washed up.

Coming back into the room, he looked to where Maggie was trying to comfort the baby, who was still fussing. Worry lines creased her face.

Catching sight of him, she met his gaze. "Now what?"

Jake hesitated, then said, "Perhaps she's hungry."

Maggie sighed. "I didn't think about that." Looking at the baby, then at Jake, she said, "I'm not sure..."

"I can't help you here, Maggie-May. I imagine if you just put her up there, she'll know what to do."

Maggie's cheeks were bright pink. She nodded.

Jake's own cheeks were warm. "I'll just go in the other room and give you some privacy," he said.

Maggie nodded, relief plainly written on her features.

Jake turned and took one step toward the kitchen, before the lights all went out.

"Jake?" Maggie's voice cut through the darkness.

He paused. "Seems I don't have to leave after all. The hurricane took care of that for us."

Chapter Twenty

The pounding on the door woke her.

Maggie rolled over in bed and groggily looked toward the window. Gray light peeked in through the pulled blinds.

Surprised, Maggie blinked. Hadn't she just finished feeding Alyssa again?

Voices in the other room drew her attention and memories came flooding back. The hurricane. It had been awful last night, keeping them up until early this morning. Alyssa had eaten twice and Jake had finally insisted she go to bed...

Oh, no, she thought mournfully, remembering other things, too, like what she'd confessed to him about her ex-fiancé.

"Maggie?"

The tap on the door jerked her gaze to it. The handle turned and Jake poked his head in. His smile faded as he studied her.

"I'm not sure what is going on behind those eyes of yours, Maggie-May, but we'll discuss it later. Rand and Elizabeth are here. The group at the cabin was worried and each took a different road home, hoping to pass us somewhere. Rand spotted my car in a ditch about a quarter of mile up the road, where the wind blew it last night, and eventually found us."

Maggie forced a smile. "I'm glad."

"Maggie?" Elizabeth's soft voice came from the other room, then the short pert redhead was pushing her way past Jake and into the room. "Oh! You had your baby!"

"What?" Rand's voice from the living room echoed Elizabeth's and then he was pushing his way into the room.

Elizabeth moved up next to Maggie. "How are you? Any problems? How's the bleeding?"

Maggie sank down into the bed, pulling the covers up to her chin at Elizabeth's very medical attack. Rand, obviously coming to the conclusion that everything was okay, smiled apologetically and backed out of the room. "Don't hassle her, Lizabeth. Just check her out and then let's get them back to civilization."

"I'm fine," Maggie protested.

"Let her help you, honey," Jake said softly.

Maggie's cheeks turned a fiery red when Rand gaped at Jake's endearment, and Elizabeth positively beamed.

"Shoo, Jake. Let me take care of her," Elizabeth said, grinning.

Maggie watched as Elizabeth shoved him out the door and closed it.

"He's in love with you," Elizabeth said, and giggled.

Maggie shrugged, thinking of everything that had happened in the past twenty-four hours. "Not in love so much as feeling responsible after delivering my baby."

Elizabeth gaped only for a minute before she came over and started examining Maggie. As she checked her tummy and poked and prodded, she said, "Why'd the chicken cross the road?"

Maggie had heard all about Elizabeth's jokes. "I don't have to answer that, do I?"

Elizabeth chuckled. "Some chickens are just so stubborn you can't teach them to stop crossing that darned road...."

Elizabeth pulled back the sheet. "Don't be stubborn, Maggie. Accept that Jake cares for you."

"I'm not stubborn," Maggie whispered when Elizabeth reached out to help her up. "I'm scared. You don't understand. My parents will cause problems."

Elizabeth left Maggie on the edge of the bed and retrieved her robe and slippers. Then she went over to check the baby. "Your parents don't control you, Maggie. You're a grown woman."

Maggie nodded as she worked her arms into the sleeves of her robe. "I know that, but my parents are angry with me about the child. They see this as some power play or something. I will come to my senses and come home. To make sure, they have found out each place I've gotten a job and ended up getting me fired."

Elizabeth picked up the baby like a pro. Pausing,

she turned to look at Maggie incredulously. "How can they do that?"

Maggie shrugged. "They hire people to find out things. My parents are stubborn. They believe I played and should pay."

Maggie motioned at the child. "They have no desire to listen to anything I have said. When they find out I've had Alyssa and plan to keep her, they'll have a fit. And they'll do anything they can to make sure I understand I have to give up my child or move out of town."

"But why?"

"I've humiliated them," she said simply.

Elizabeth wrapped the baby in a blanket, handed her to Maggie and then began picking up. "Jake won't allow them to hurt you, Maggie."

"They'll find something that matters to him, something to hold over his head. I can't let that happen."

Elizabeth finished cleaning up, then repacked Maggie's suitcase. "Maggie, hon, you've got to stop playing God. Trust Him to do His job."

Maggie didn't comment but hugged Alyssa, comforting her until she stopped crying. "How is she?" Maggie asked.

"Just fine, as are you. There's a bit of tearing, but other than that, you're fine. You'll need to go to a doctor and let him examine you."

Maggie stood and moved to the bathroom.

Elizabeth followed.

"I'm fine, Elizabeth, really," Maggie said as she ran a brush through her hair and cleaned her face and teeth.

"I'm sure you are. However, I'll just stick by you in case."

Maggie finished up and hobbled back into the room. She went over to Alyssa, picked her up and cuddled her.

"She's a beautiful baby, Maggie."

Elizabeth's soft words caught her attention, and she glanced around to see Elizabeth staring at Alyssa.

"God gives us good out of disasters sometimes," Maggie murmured.

Realizing what she had said, she glanced up at Elizabeth. Instead of shock, she saw understanding. "Yes, He does, Maggie."

Elizabeth went to the door. "Okay, guys, we're ready."

Jake came in and headed right for Maggie.

"Can you walk out to the car, Maggie?"

"I'm not an invalid," she whispered low, her cheeks pink.

Jake nodded. "You've more than proven that, sweetheart."

Maggie silently groaned at his words.

Rand collected the suitcases and left the room, chuckling as he did. Elizabeth followed, offering Rand advice on just where to put the suitcases in the car.

"Are they always like that?" Maggie asked, watching the couple leave. She thought it was a good way to turn the subject away from her so Jake wouldn't continue with his mothering.

Jake gave her a knowing smile, indicating he understood exactly what she was doing. "Like what, Maggie-May?"

"She's so full of energy, bouncing around him, offering suggestions. And Rand simply smiles and nods, never getting the least bit bent out of shape over all her advice."

Jake chuckled. "Oh, that. Yes, Rand is pretty easygoing when it comes to his wife. Of course, I can see why he'd be that way if he loved her."

Jake looked into Maggie's eyes.

Maggie's heart flip-flopped at the tender expression in his eyes. "How can you love me, Jake?" she murmured, realizing exactly what he was thinking. "Especially after everything you know?"

Maggie adjusted the baby in her arms.

Jake cupped Maggie's cheek. "Bad things happen to us all, Maggie-May. It's how we handle them that tells what type of character we have. You're strong. I wish the violence had never happened, but it did and you survived. I'm outraged. If I ever meet the guy, I'd liked to smash his nose for him. It's going to take me a lot of time and prayer before I can ever forgive what that person did to you. But we both have to heal. And I want to be there for you because I love you, Maggie. I love you more than I ever thought possible."

"Oh, Jake," Maggie murmured, tears coming to her eyes. "And I love you, too. More than I know how to express."

Jake rubbed her cheek before allowing his hand to slip around to the base of her neck and urging her forward for a kiss.

Maggie leaned into his kiss, meeting his lips with her own. His were firm, strong and yet tender as they caressed her. Maggie sighed against his mouth returning the kiss.

When Jake pulled back, all the love he felt glowed in his eyes. "Maggie, darlin', will you marry me?"

Maggie stared, overwhelmed by Jake's question.

Marriage. Oh, how she loved this man. But marriage?

She thought of all the problems in the past year, of the things she'd gone through. She realized now she had never truly loved her ex-fiancé. No, she had cared deeply for him, but she had never loved him with the deep abiding love that tied two souls together under God.

She did love this man like that.

And he loved her and Alyssa, and didn't care about the past. Could she actually have found a satisfying ending to the mess of the past year after all?

Seeing the love in Jake's eyes, she melted. "Oh, yes, Jake," she whispered.

Leaning against him, she wept.

"Shh, Maggie, hon. I didn't mean to make you cry."

Maggie chuckled through her tears. "I don't know how I got so lucky."

"It's that Irish name your parents gave you," he joked.

Hearing her parents mentioned burst the euphoric bubble and brought reality crashing back in. "Jake. What will your church say? I mean, I don't have the most sterling reputation...."

Jake frowned at her. "Maggie, you have to get over that."

"But what will they say? I don't want to hurt your career."

Jake shook his head. "You have to let God take care of things, Maggie. Stop trying to control everything. If you look in the Bible, you'll discover the people in there weren't perfect. Stop examining something that wasn't your fault. If God forgave people for their sometimes bad choices and used them for His glory, how can you worry about something that isn't your fault?"

Maggie smiled through her tears, thinking Jake was one of a kind. "Thank you."

Jake returned the smile. "It was a violent crime, Maggie. Violence is something we can't control. Don't ever let anyone tell you that you were responsible. You hear me?"

Maggie nodded. "I—I'm just worried that something more disastrous is going to happen—"

Jake covered her lips with a finger, then leaned in and replaced it with his lips. When he finally broke the kiss, he smiled at her gently. "Enough. Trust God, Maggie."

Maggie nodded, wanting to believe what Jake was saying. Slowly she allowed her hope to build, her joy to replace her fear.

"Now, Maggie, darlin', is your answer still yes? Because let me warn you, you've already said yes and I won't let you go back on your word now."

Maggie smiled. "How can I refuse?"

Jake grinned, self-satisfied. "Is that so. I'll remember that, then."

He pulled Maggie into his arms and gave her a bear hug.

Alyssa squawked.

Jake released Maggie and looked down at the child—their child, as far as he was concerned. "Did I hurt her?"

Maggie shook her head and glanced shyly up at Jake. "She's probably getting hungry."

A throat clearing at the door of the bedroom intruded on the intimate setting and Jake turned. Rand stood there.

"Congratulations. I didn't mean to interrupt."

Jake shook his head. "You didn't. And thanks for the well-wishes. I don't think anything could make me feel happier than Maggie agreeing to be my wife, though."

Elizabeth squealed and ran forward to hug Maggie and then Jake. Rand shook his hand and then kissed Maggie on the cheek.

Jake was the first to break up the happy scene. "Alyssa is hungry and Maggie is tired. Let's get them to the car and back to Centerton."

Rand's smile faded. "And see what is left of our town?"

Jake's own smile faded. "Yeah."

Reality impinged. However, Jake found, despite the reality, there was still a buoyancy in his spirit, a joy that knowing, no matter what he found back in Centerton, he had his future right here with him.

Chapter Twenty-One

"**Y**ou look tired."

Maggie turned from the church kitchen, where she was making more sandwiches to deliver to a local shelter in the community. "I'm fine, Jake."

Jake moved over and rubbed her shoulders. "How's Alyssa?"

Maggie glanced to where the baby slept in a bassinet borrowed from the nursery. "Sleeping again."

"You should be, too," Jake murmured.

Maggie leaned back against Jake, enjoying his strength and gentleness as he held her. "I only wanted to get a few more sandwiches made before the crew gets back."

"And you have. Now, go rest. Remember, the doctor told you to rest these past two weeks."

Maggie turned in Jake's arms and hugged him. "I know. I know. And I am...."

Jake chuckled and squeezed Maggie. "You are now."

Maggie sighed, resting in Jake's arms, looking at Alyssa. She hadn't been this happy for a long time. Life was good, except for one small thing.

"Have you called your parents yet?"

Jake's low voice rumbled against where her ear was pressed to his chest.

Her parents.

"No."

Jake didn't comment, only squeezed Maggie tighter. Anxiety crept into Maggie as she thought about her parents. "I can't tell them, Jake."

"You can't *not* tell them, Maggie. You have to heal. As long as you hold on to the past and the fear, you can't heal and go on."

Maggie's chest tightened, and she pushed back. Looking up into his eyes, she whispered, "You don't understand. They don't approve. There is nothing I will be able to say that will change that. As far as they're concerned, I'm an embarrassment." They'll hurt you, she silently whispered her fear.

"They've had time, Maggie, to change their mind. However, I'm not asking you to do this for them. I want you to do this for you. Face them. See that there isn't anything they can do that will run you off this time. I'll be there with you."

Maggie's heart raced. "Why do you keep insisting I face them? Can't we just marry and…and…"

When she didn't continue, Jake cupped her cheek. "It's better to get the situation out in the open and get it over with so we can start our marriage on fresh ground. And I don't want to sneak around behind them, Maggie. You've got to face them…and heal. Face the past and your fears, and then we can go on.''

Maggie heard his words but shook her head. ''You don't understand. We've been through this a thousand times in the past two weeks, Jake. They'll find something to manipulate us with. They're angry that I was going to have this child. I would just as soon not see them rather than risk things being—''

Jake pulled her back into his arms and hugged her. Whispering gently, he said, ''I'm sorry I pushed you. But I think you're wrong. What could your parents possibly do that could cause us problems?''

Maggie didn't want to venture a guess. Since meeting Jake she realized her parents were hurting and by forcing her away they could deny their own pain. Knowing that, though, didn't change what they'd try to do…which would be to make Maggie bend to their will again. At Jake's expense.

If only they had believed her…

''Let's get you and Alyssa back to your house so you can—''

''Margaret?''

Maggie stiffened.

Jake, hearing the soft feminine voice, stepped back from Maggie and turned in the direction of the voice. An older woman and gentleman stood before him…people who were very familiar to him. ''Henry. Mary.'' Jake nodded at the Hendersons, wondering what had brought them here. ''Maggie, this is Henry and Mary Henderson, who are on the board of directors—''

"Mom? Dad?"

Jake looked sharply at Maggie. Her eyes were wide with shock and her face pale. His gaze shot back to two people he had been working with the past year. They were pale, too, standing there staring at Maggie like—

When Mary's gaze went to the bassinet and jerked away, he asked, "These are your parents?"

Maggie nodded.

Jake reached out for her to guide her back in his arms, but Maggie pulled away. Slowly her back straightened and all emotion left her face. Coolly, she asked, "What are you doing here?"

Jake ached for Maggie. He'd seen the glimpse of fear. Silently he berated himself for not finding out sooner just who her parents were. "Maggie, your parents and I work together, sweetheart. I'm sure they're only here—"

"'Sweetheart'?"

Jake turned toward Mary, who had sounded absolutely appalled. "Mary—"

"I see she's sucked you into her lies, too, Jake," Mary said.

Oh, boy, Jake thought. Automatically, he moved closer to Maggie. "Why don't we all go into my office and sit down where we can—"

"She's good at that," Mary interrupted, overriding Jake. "How many other people have you lied to, Margaret, and told that you were leaving the area, only to turn up again? How many people did you tell lies to so you could hide around here and try to manipulate us into accepting the life-style you've chosen?"

"It's not a life-style, Mom. I told you—"

"You refused to marry Chester. What type of life-style would you call that—sleeping around, getting caught and then refusing to do the right thing? And then walking around proud of the fact that you're a single parent. After all we've done for you, and you won't even leave the area...."

"Excuse me," Jake said, appalled at the attack Mary had launched against her own daughter. "Let's just go to my office." Jake hoped that once there he could calm the Hendersons down and they could all talk.

"Well?" Henry asked his daughter, ignoring Jake. "Isn't it enough your mother lost nights of sleep over your revenge as you flouted our failure? And now we find out you're hanging around this pastor, making a mockery of everything he is trying to do?"

"Just a minute here," Jake began. "Henry, Mary, I welcome you into the church, but I won't allow you to go around attacking its members or my future wife."

Shocked silence fell.

"Your...wife?" Henry sounded as if he were choking.

Mary stared aghast. "But—"

Maggie touched Jake's arm. "Jake, please..."

Jake knew he wasn't handling this well, but hearing what they had said to Maggie infuriated him. "Yes. I've asked Maggie to marry me." Jake smiled, though he was absolutely furious inside. "So, why don't we go into the office and discuss this like civilized humans?"

He immediately knew he'd said the wrong thing by the Hendersons' narrow-eyed look.

"You have no idea what you've gotten yourself into, Jake Mathison. Or maybe you do," Mary said scathingly. "This child of ours has done her best to rebel against us. We have simply been trying to practice tough love and get her straightened out. Instead, you come along and give her shelter."

"Mom!" Maggie said, dismayed.

"Is that so," Jake said mildly. "What did you think to do by banning her from your house and making sure she had no job?"

Henry moved up to Mary. "We thought to let her see what real life is like. How tough it can be. Until she recognizes what she has done is wrong and will accept and apologize to us...."

"Wrong?"

"Jake," Maggie pleaded, touching his arm.

Jake immediately turned to her. When he saw the tears in her eyes, his anger deflated and his mind cleared. Slipping a hand to her back, he rubbed gently. "I'm sorry, Maggie. Get Alyssa and we'll go to my office and all sit down and talk."

Maggie shook her head. Turning, she faced her parents. "Look, I love you both, Mom, Dad, but I don't want to fight anymore. I have a baby now and am making a life for myself. Can't you just stop?"

Henry scowled. "If you'd come home and act like a daughter and stop spreading lies about Chester, sure we could. But you keep placing all the blame for your actions everywhere else. All we want, girl, is for you to take some responsibility in this and then we'll support you."

Jake felt his temper rising again. *Father, give me wisdom to know what to say,* he prayed. *And peace,* he thought.

"Enough," he said in a low voice to Maggie's parents. "If you have something to say, we'll go into my office and discuss it. But there will be no more arguing in the kitchen here."

Maggie's parents stiffened up like fireplace pokers and their looks could have frozen the flames of Hell they were so cold.

"Come on, Mary," Henry said. "This is ridiculous. You were right."

"We'll just see what the board has to say about Jake's judgment," Mary hissed at Maggie.

"What do you mean by that?" Maggie asked, fear leaping to her features.

Mary smiled with smug satisfaction. "Well, if Jake can't handle his own church or what type of people he hires to work here, he surely can't be in charge of this project. We'll pull our support immediately, and after everyone else hears about his inability to judge rationally, I'm sure the others will follow."

Her parents strode out of the kitchen. Maggie felt sick as her greatest fears were realized. Jake was now going to pay the price for what she'd done. "I'm so sorry, Jake. I...I..."

Jake watched Maggie's parents go before turning to Maggie. "Why didn't you tell me who your parents were? You go by the last name Garderé."

"I didn't want anyone to know."

Jake sighed and then rubbed at his neck. "Great."

Maggie studied him, nauseated. "What are you going to do? They're very angry and bitter and blame me for this whole situation."

"I would have never guessed." Jake shook his head, disgusted. "I can tell you one thing, though. They aren't going to destroy that center. I've worked too hard for this. I don't care what it takes—I'm going to see it finished. I should probably call Tyler and Gage and let them know what's happening, just in case your parents do decide to spread slander. I'll be back in a bit."

With a sinking feeling Maggie watched Jake stride out of the room. Jake was going to lose the center because her parents held a grudge against her and were going to use him to prove a point.

Slowly Maggie shook her head. Not this time. This time she'd let them win. This time she would leave, because she loved Jake.

Chapter Twenty-Two

Jake rubbed wearily at his forehead. He'd been at his desk for three hours going over the paperwork for the lumber prices. His figures were right. There was no way, if Maggie's parents pulled their bid, they could meet their budget and get the building done.

Why hadn't she told him?

"Knock, knock."

Jake looked up to see Tyler standing at the door. At six foot two, Tyler tended to tower in doorways. A big man, with a heart of gold. "Come on in, Tyler," Jake said, waving a hand.

Tyler ambled in and seated himself across from Jake. "So, Jake. What have you found?" Tyler made a gesture at the paperwork on Jake's desk.

"If they pull their bid, we can't afford it." Jake sighed and rubbed at his neck. "I just don't understand why Maggie didn't tell me sooner who her parents were."

Tyler frowned. Jake hadn't told him what had happened to Maggie, only that her parents had tossed out an ultimatum and she had chosen not to follow it. "Seems to me the girl was scared. I mean, the only time you don't tell someone where you are is if you're hiding."

Jake nodded. "Yeah, she was hiding. She was worried that her parents would try something exactly like this if they found out where she was."

Tyler shook his head. "Such a shame her parents can't let go of her and let her run her own life. Some parents are that way."

Jake straightened the paperwork and stuffed it back into the folder. "I've counseled enough to know that. I don't understand why Maggie can't let go of the pain her parents caused and just let herself heal. You should have seen her earlier. Her whole face froze with fear when her parents showed up. And things went downhill from there."

When Tyler didn't comment, Jake glanced up. Seeing Tyler studying him, he cocked his head curiously. "What?"

"You know, Jake, you're taking this attack awfully personally. I realize you love the building project, but why aren't you out there with Maggie, comforting her, instead of going over these papers?"

Jake looked down at the papers and then at Jake. "I just wanted to try to stop any damage her parents might be about to cause."

"Why? Isn't it you who always preaches that God will take care of things if we trust Him? Why is it so important that you handle this?"

Jake saw what Tyler was getting at, and knew Tyler was right. "My brother's death."

Tyler nodded. "I know, Jake, you always wanted to do this for him. But, I think this building project has become an obsession to you, so much so that you've forgotten God is the one who is in charge of this, not you. Perhaps you should practice what you told Maggie and do a little healing yourself."

Jake felt a pang in his heart. "I just wanted to see that place built, for my brother."

Tyler shook his head. "No, Jake. I think the place is for you. You weren't there for him when he needed you and so by doing this you're atoning. Perhaps you should try forgiving yourself, since God...and your brother...forgave you years ago."

Jake's shoulders drooped. Looking back, he realized suddenly that Tyler was right. All these years he'd had in the back of his mind that he needed to get this place built for kids to go. It'd become an obsession to him, a need that outweighed everything. *Forgive me, Father, for not seeing this sooner*, he prayed.

"I even put it before Maggie," Jake whispered. Turning to Tyler, he continued, "Instead of staying and supporting her when she needed it, I rushed back here to try to save the project."

Tyler sighed. "We all make mistakes. Why don't you knock off, go find Maggie and apologize. Leave this in God's hands."

Peace flowed through Jake. "You're right. I've been such an idiot."

Healing flooded his heart as he realized that

through all these years he had been holding in a pain of loss and blaming himself. There was no reason he should have held that in the way he had. He should have let it go, let God heal him and accepted that there was nothing he could have done.

As he accepted that now, Maggie's parents' threats faded. So what if they tried to smear his name? There would be time to build this. If it was God's will, a door would open up with funds for the lumber or another place even less inexpensive to buy lumber from.

"You're right, Tyler. If Gage calls, tell him I've gone home for the evening."

Tyler smiled. "Good."

Jake nodded. "Thanks, Tyler."

Jake owed Maggie an apology for running off like he did.

She wasn't in the kitchen and Alyssa was gone. He checked the nursery, too. It was only as he approached her house that something niggled at him. Something was different.

He jogged up the steps and knocked on the door. "Maggie?"

He waited.

She didn't answer.

Jake winced, realizing his inattention might have actually hurt her. Knocking louder he called out, "Maggie-May, open up, please."

Still she didn't answer.

Worry touched his spine. He hesitated only a moment before pulling the screen door back and checking the other door. It opened easily under his hand.

He stepped in and looked around.

"Maggie?"

He walked into the house and headed toward the kitchen. The sight in the bedroom stopped him and he backtracked.

Dread built in his chest when he noted all the open drawers and empty cabinets. "Maggie!"

He hurried to Alyssa's room and discovered the same condition.

"Her car."

He realized her car wasn't in the driveway.

Running back into the living room, he looked out.

He whirled and went to the kitchen, hoping, praying, Maggie had simply found a new place to live and had forgotten to mention it to him.

The piece of paper on the table told him he was wrong.

Jake,
I couldn't stay. I had to go. I'm sorry for the problems I've caused. When my parents find I am gone, they'll back off and the center will be saved. God bless you for all you've done. My love,

Maggie

Jake rubbed at a stain on the paper before realizing that the ink was blurred by Maggie's tears.

"Mmmmeeewww."

Jake looked down to see Captain Kat winding her way around his feet, whining at the loss of Maggie.

"Why didn't you wait, Maggie, and let me explain? Why didn't you ask me just what meant more to me?"

Fear.

That was the simple answer.

Maggie had never had the chance to heal herself. How was she to know what he felt? Maggie had had so many people put their wants and needs first that it would be very easy for her to think Jake just might do that. "But it didn't mean that much, Maggie. You mean more to me, so much more."

As he stood there and read the note, he realized that because of his own inability to let go of the past and heal, he had just lost the only woman he would ever love.

Chapter Twenty-Three

Maggie trudged along the road toward home and Alyssa. The small town of Luvilla, Louisiana, had a transportation system, but it wasn't all that great. Looking up at the cloudy sky, Maggie had to wonder if she was going to get soaked before she made it the four blocks to her home.

Maggie smiled, thinking of her three-month-old daughter and how chunky she'd gotten. It was hard to believe that she was the same tiny child Maggie gave birth to.

Thinking of that birth reminded Maggie of Jake, which reminded her of what she had left behind. Melancholy settled over her.

Jake.

Her heart felt as if there were a gaping hole where he had once been. How she missed him. She had debated only for a short while before leaving and head-ing north. It had been God who had landed her the secretarial job in the small city near Alexandria.

She firmly believed that. Stopping at that diner to eat had been divine guidance. The waitress's brother was a lawyer, who just so happened to need a secretary because his was leaving on Friday.

She'd been hired within the hour.

In a way, Maggie hated how it had worked out. She had thought about going back and talking to Jake, but with the job, she hadn't had time. On several occasions she'd picked up the phone to call and explain. She'd even thought to write.

Truth was, she just couldn't bring herself to do it.

A drop of rain hit Maggie on the cheek.

Glancing up, she saw the dark skies and sighed. Looked as if she was going to get wet again. Ducking her head, she hurried along, intent on arriving home as quickly as possible to keep from getting completely soaked.

So intent was she on her path that it was a moment before she noticed the car that had pulled up beside her. Before she had a chance to look up, an achingly familiar voice said softly, "Need a ride, Maggie-May?"

Stunned, she stopped and stared at Jake. He still looked as ruggedly handsome as ever, though there were circles under his eyes. She blinked, but he was still there when she opened her eyes.

"What are you doing here?" she asked, trembling, certain he was going to disappear any moment.

He smiled. "Hunting for you."

Her heart soared. Breathing became downright hard. "How'd you find me?"

Jake's eyes twinkled. "Do you know a woman named Thelma at the local diner?"

"Yes," she whispered.

"She was nice enough to call me and tell me to get up here and heal your broken heart."

"She didn't!" Maggie said, stunned.

Jake got out, took Maggie by the elbow and led her around to the other door. "I'm afraid so, honey. I'm going to name our second child after her."

"What?" Maggie stared at Jake, wondering if he'd grown two heads.

Leaning down, he kissed her gently. "I love you. We're going to be married. But first—"

He closed the door and went back around to his side of the car; he climbed in just as it really started raining. Pulling the door shut, he turned to look at her. "I have to apologize, Maggie. I should never have left you that day to go see about the building project. I should have stayed and made sure you were okay."

Maggie shook her head. "No, Jake. I understand. That building project meant everything to you."

Jake slowly nodded. "Yes, it did. That's why I resigned as the head of the committee and turned things over to Tyler."

"You what?" Maggie gripped Jake's arm. "What did my parents do? I'm so sorry! I—"

Jake leaned over and kissed her again. Grinning, he said, "That's a good way to quiet you."

Turning serious, he continued, "Your parents

opened my eyes. That's what they did. When they
came and confronted you, and Tyler made me see
how worried I was over the building project, I realized I'd never allowed myself to heal. God can handle
that. I am only in an advisory position now, if I decide
to accept it.''

"If? I don't understand, Jake. What do you
mean?''

Jake stroked Maggie's cheek. "I also told the el-
ders of the church that I might be resigning. It all
depends on you. If you don't want to go back to the
area where your parents live, then we'll leave. However, before you decide, I think you should know
some things.''

Jake pulled out a letter and newspaper clipping and
handed them to Maggie. "Your ex-fiancé was ar-
rested the other day for attempted rape and assault.
Seems he got drunk and tried to force himself on
another woman.''

Maggie shook as she took the article and read it.
"And this?'' she asked, opening the letter.

"From your parents, Maggie. It appears they are
despondent over what they've done. They came to me
and apologized and said that if you contacted me to
please tell you that they wanted to talk to you and
apologize to you for ever doubting you. They also
want to tell you that they love you and hope one day
you can find it in your heart to forgive them.''

Maggie began to cry.

"Ah, Maggie, darlin','' Jake said softly, and pulled
her into his arms. She rested there, listening to his
soothing voice, and cried out all the pain, the hurt,

the distrust of the past year and allowed her Heavenly Father to slowly replace the pain with peace.

When she finally pulled back from Jake, the rain was coming down in sheets.

Jake stroked her cheek. "I love you."

Fresh tears sprang to her eyes. "And I love you. I've been such a fool."

"No, never, Maggie," Jake whispered. "It took your leaving for all this to come about. God's timing, not ours. Remember that. Things always work out in His time."

Maggie nodded.

His eyes connected with and held hers. "So, do I start looking for another church or do you want to come back?"

"You'd do that for me?"

Jake nodded, deadly serious. "That and more, Maggie, if it meant keeping you at my side."

Maggie slowly shook her head. "No, Jake. God comes first. If He wants you at that church, who am I to gainsay Him? I'll go back."

Jake leaned forward. A inch from her lips, he paused. "And marry me, and live with me until we're old and gray and rocking in rockers on the front porch? And help me take care of Captain Kat, who has taken to sleeping with me every night."

A slow smile curved Maggie's mouth. "Oh, dear!"

Jake laughed. "Yeah. Oh, dear."

"I'll have fifty great-grandchildren running circles around us, and twenty cats sleeping with us, Jake, as long as I'm with you."

"Good."

With a smug smile of satisfaction, Jake sealed the bargain with a kiss.

* * * * *

Dear Reader,

Sometimes in life we feel all alone, having gone through some pain or hurt that we think no one else can understand. Or sometimes don't want to understand. Such is the case for Maggie, the heroine in this story, who has gone through a very traumatic experience and is trying to pick up the pieces of her life and go on.

It takes Jake to teach her that the love of Jesus can heal all hurts, while learning that lesson all over for himself. God loves us, wants us to heal, to let go of the past and the pain. Sometimes, as Christians, we get so caught up in what is right or wrong that we forget that we're supposed to love and help each other, be there for one another, not condemn.

I hope, if you've been hurt in the past (and who of us hasn't?) that this story will touch your heart and open you up again to God's healing love as you travel the road of rediscovery with Maggie and Jake in *A Mother's Love*. Please write me and let me know what you think. I love to hear from readers. P.O. Box 207, Slaughter, LA 70777.

In Christ's Love,

Cheryl Wolverton

Take 2 inspirational love stories FREE!

PLUS get a FREE surprise gift!

Special Limited-Time Offer

Mail to Steeple Hill Reader Service™

In U.S.	In Canada
3010 Walden Ave.	P.O. Box 609
P.O. Box 1867	Fort Erie, Ontario
Buffalo, NY 14240-1867	L2A 5X3

YES! Please send me 2 free Love Inspired® novels and my free surprise gift. Then send me 3 brand-new novels every month, which I will receive months before they appear in bookstores. Bill me at the low price of $3.74 each in the U.S. and $3.96 each in Canada, plus 25¢ delivery and applicable sales tax, if any*. That's the complete price and a saving of over 10% off the cover prices—quite a bargain! I understand that accepting the books and gift places me under no obligation ever to buy any books. I can always return a shipment and cancel at any time. Even if I never buy another book from Steeple Hill, the 2 free books and the surprise gift are mine to keep forever.

303 IEN CM6R
103 IEN CM6Q

Name	(PLEASE PRINT)
Address	Apt. No.
City	State/Prov. Zip/Postal Code

* Terms and prices are subject to change without notice. Sales tax applicable in New York. Canadian residents will be charged applicable provincial taxes and GST. All orders subject to approval. Offer limited to one per household.

INTLI-299

©1998

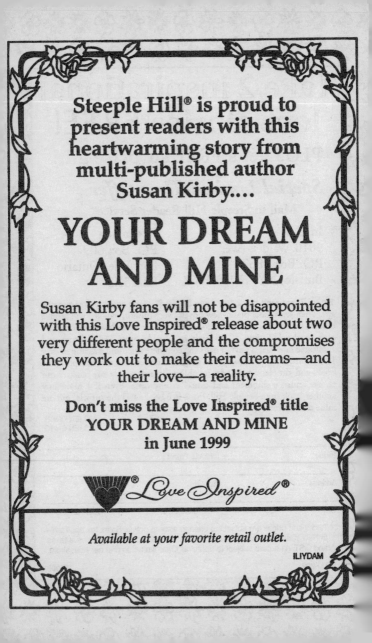